THE STORY
THEY NEVER
TELL US

THE STORY THEY NEVER TELL US

BRENNA BLAYLOCK

NEW DEGREE PRESS

THE STORY THEY NEVER TELL US

ISBN   978-1-63676-468-9   *Paperback*

            978-1-63676-469-6   *Kindle Ebook*

            978-1-63676-470-2   *Ebook*

Dedication

To my Diggity Dog members, never change.

CONTENTS

———

"*The only way to deal with an unfree world is to become so absolutely free that your very existence is an act of rebellion.*"

—ALBERT CAMUS*

AUTHOR'S NOTE

———

Dear Readers,

I am privileged. Although, privilege for a Black woman does not mean the same as it does for others. I became acutely aware of limitations to my freedom when I was introduced to microaggressions at the fragile age of four. Growing up in White America, I was not allowed to experience the beauty of innocence that is tied with youth. As a privileged Black child, I was *still* given the talk about how to encounter the police in order to get home safe. As a Black girl, I was told by my parents that my hair and darker complexion were beautiful. My parents begged for me to believe their words, knowing every institution in America would teach me otherwise. I hope one day our country acknowledges the antiblack narrative cemented in our society, leaving a small space for the ignorant paradigm to shift.

Discriminatory and racist issues do not only involve police brutality—a question of a higher mortality rate. Survival is not only returning home, but also attempting to navigate a world that was never meant for you to be successful in. I hope to progress to a productive, cohesive society which depends on America's willingness to take accountability for our brutal history. Throughout this book, *The Story They Never Tell Us,* I pull from my own experiences of oppression, cultural appropriation, and discrimination while attending a predominately White institution (PWI) through Aaliyah's viewpoint. I explore the "systemic states of America" with a take on the PWI experience for Black students. Through Aaliyah, readers will go on a journey experiencing the aloof encounters of institutionalized racism in professional spaces. This book was made to teach those that are willing to learn their ignorance while also assisting Black students to transition to higher education.

NOBODY TELLS YOU: MOVE-IN DAY

————

Aaliyah Harris taped up her last box. She shifted her knees on her suitcase to zip it up. She released a long breath as the moment became nostalgic.

"You ready for your brothers to come take your things to the car?" Aaliyah's father's bald head glowed in the afternoon light, but his smile was even brighter.

"Yeah, I just zipped up my luggage."

John Harris sauntered down the carpeted hall, and in the distance, Aaliyah heard him say, "Boys, be ready to get your sister's luggage in five minutes."

Aaliyah chuckled at their unison response, "Yes sir."

Aaliyah scanned her room. Placed behind her bed frame were pink, blue, and purple nuance posters of all her favorite artists. Surrounding the posters of artists were three posters from her favorite show *The Boondocks*, which in bold letters read, "REVOLT," "VISION," and "RISE." She unplugged the lights on her wall that remained light pink for the last month. The room looked lifeless without the pink complimenting her posters. She ran her hand along the faded Angela Davis portrait her sister gave her when she was eight.

"It'll be here when you get back."

Aaliyah's older sister, Keisha, appeared in the doorway leaning on her right side. She stared at her younger sister while the sun glistened on her face. Aaliyah saw so much of herself in her older sister—and she wanted it that way.

Aaliyah turned around to her sister, "I know my records won't be though."

Keisha laughed, showing all her perfect teeth. "Oh, for sure. Damien will be in that record box the minute the car starts." Their sentimental moment was interrupted by their brothers barging into Aaliyah's room.

"Is that it?" Damien, Aaliyah's older brother by two years, pointed at the four boxes placed by Aaliyah's floor lamp.

Ty picked up a box before Aaliyah answered Damien's question. The box almost blocked his eight-year-old view.

Aaliyah placed her alarm clock on top of the stacked boxes. "Now it is. I'll roll my luggage out soon."

Damien gave Aaliyah a nod. He grabbed the remaining items and disappeared into the hall. Damien's build resembled their dad's in his twenties—six foot three and muscular.

"Now *what* am I going to do with macho meathead over there while you're gone? I need to protect Ty from his ways." Keisha winced while Aaliyah laughed.

"You'll do the same thing I did when you went off to Berkeley—survive." Aaliyah wrapped her arm around Keisha's shoulders.

"Yeah," Keisha's shoulders softened as if the memories rested heavy on them, "just don't come back pregnant." Keisha gave her a dimpled smile, but her tone was stern.

Aaliyah smiled back at her sister.

"Come on girls, your mom is ready to hit the road." Their dad stuck his head in the doorframe while he helped Ty put on his jacket.

Aaliyah yanked up the handle on her suitcase and followed her family down the hallway. She walked outside to see Damien rearranging her mattress in their 2009 Corolla. She wheeled her suitcase and stopped two inches short of his feet.

"Just because you're leaving don't mean your arms are broke," Damien said to Aaliyah as she was walking away. She turned around with a witty comeback on her tongue but was beat by her dad's swift hand to the back of Damien's head. "Boy."

Damien rubbed the spot that was hit, "My bad, Dad."

Aaliyah chuckled and leaned into her dad's arms as he engulfed her in a hug. She was five foot ten, but her father's six-foot-four build made her feel small and protected.

"Do you have everything?" Tina Harris came out the house in a mint-green sundress that faded into a baby blue.

"Girl, you know you fine!" Aaliyah's father walked past his wife and smacked her behind. Their kids rolled their eyes while Aaliyah's mother shook her head with a faint smile.

"Okay, say your goodbyes." Aaliyah knew her mother was emotional. The sun reflected against the well up in her eyes.

Damien slammed the trunk shut and ran at Aaliyah in his linebacker position he once played in football. "Come here!" He scooped her up and tossed her over his shoulders. "My little sister is going to college! My little sister is going to college! My little sister is going to college!" he sang off key.

Aaliyah shouted in between laughs, "Damien!" She lightly punched him on his back, then he set her down gently.

"Love you. Be safe. I better not see you with no boyfriend or I'm coming up there."

Aaliyah rolled her eyes at his affection, "Love you too."

Aaliyah's dad was next. He wrapped Aaliyah up in a hug and kissed her ear. She giggled as he rubbed the scruff of his beard all over her face, something she's loved since she was a baby. "My baby's going to college. My baby's going to college. My baby's going to college," he sang to the same tune of Damien's song but on key. "I'm sorry they wouldn't let me off work today, baby girl. You know I tried." He looked at her collarbone, disappointedly not meeting her eyes.

Aaliyah tilted her head up to look her father in the eye, "I know you tried. I love you to the moon."

He perked up, "And I love you to the milky way."

Keisha stood behind their father. She was staring at Aaliyah for a few seconds, and her breathing became labored. She said through hiccups of unshed tears, "I'm really gonna miss you." She released a cry once Aaliyah was in her arms.

Aaliyah rubbed her older sister's back for a moment. "Keisha, I love you, but I don't want to mess up my first-day-of-school outfit." Aaliyah laughed while slightly pulling away from her weeping sister.

"Girl, your first day of school is in three days," Keisha said and wiped the mascara from her cheeks. She pulled away and held both of Aaliyah's hands. "You're stepping into your greatness that I and everybody else see. I love you. Have so much fun."

Aaliyah couldn't respond over the lump in her throat, so she smiled.

John, Damien, and Keisha stood at the doorway and waved as Aaliyah climbed in the car. Ty sat in the back reading the comic book Damien gave him for the ride. Tina reached her hand over and ran her thumb across Aaliyah's knuckles. Aaliyah relaxed her clenched fists.

Four hours into the trip, Aaliyah couldn't help but notice one thing: how many Whole Foods, Trader Joe's, and Sprouts they passed by. The closest Trader Joe's to their house was thirty-five minutes away—Aaliyah had never even been inside one. The car had been pretty silent, solemn with the fact that she was departing for four months. Aaliyah abruptly broke the silence, "They have so many fancy grocery stores …" she whispered to the passenger window, "and all we have are KFCs, Popeyes, and McDonald's."

"Lord, here you go! You gonna have to tone it down, Miss X. You're going to a prestigious university, one that gave you a full ride and is ranked top ten in the state. You don't need to be worryin' about no grocery stores. Let them drink their green juice in peace."

Aaliyah looked in the rearview mirror to see Ty's perplexed face at the foreign cuisine option, "green juice." She laughed as she plugged in her phone to the aux cord and played "Today Was a Good Day" by Ice Cube. The wind picked up soon after. Aaliyah rolled up her window with a sigh. The tune played as Aaliyah shifted in her seat until her Twin XL mattress pad was no longer two centimeters from her forehead. The scenery shifted from public transportation and homeless tents to efficient stop lights and from plants in the island instead of families begging for money. Aaliyah kept her eyes on the window as she approached her new home for the next four years. Her hands were clenched once again.

Aaliyah woke up with a shake on the arm from her mom, while Ty shouted "Aaliyahhh! Let's go!" Aaliyah looked around in the dimly lit parking garage with commotion meeting her outside of their car. Her stomach turned. She hesitantly stepped out of the car, allowing her eyes to adjust to the brightness of her new surroundings. Aaliyah scanned what met them outside of the garage. She saw one family pushing their corgi in a wagon. He wagged his tail next to the Xbox, desk lamp, and shoe organizer a tall young man was pushing. The man kept his eyes on his things, ensuring they wouldn't fall, and bumped into the girl that was walking a foot in front of him. His Xbox slipped out of the wagon with his dog panting over it. The boy mumbled a quick apology as he tended to his Xbox. Aaliyah looked at herself in the passenger mirror and saw her face read far from satisfaction.

She snapped out of it. "Alright ma, you stay here. Ty and I will go get a moving bin. I'm gonna try to make sure this is one trip."

Aaliyah grabbed Ty's hand as their mother shouted behind them, "We're not coming back from the grocery store! It doesn't have to be one trip! Aali—"

Aaliyah kept her head down, embarrassed at the families looking at where the shouts were coming from. Ty's head was down as he attempted to walk on the cracks in the sidewalk. Aaliyah used their shared hand to guide him toward a large group of people. She found a young woman with dirty blonde hair, a red shirt, and a headset talking to parents and students with a chipper smile. She made eye contact with Aaliyah, "Hi, I'm Ally! If you have any questions, I am happy to help!"

"I do actually. I'm looking for…" Aaliyah pulled out her 2016 Android to look for the screenshot of her dorm name, "Wilburt Hall?"

"Perfect! Wilburt Hall is actually right behind me. You parked in the right spot. I suggest grabbing a moving bin and standing in line to get checked in so you can receive your room key."

"Great, thank you."

Aaliyah made sure she kept an eye on Ty and grabbed a neon-orange twenty-four-by-sixteen-by-eighteen-inch moving bin labeled "Wilbur Residents Only." "Go ahead Ty, lead the way back to Momma."

"Okay!" He began walking on the cracks again, this time with more confidence.

A family of four passed by with an eighty-inch plasma screen TV, a Wii, and a newly packaged white and gold dresser. Their BMW SUV was still packed full. Aaliyah looked back at their 2009 Corolla and silently began to pack up their bin.

After about thirty minutes, they managed to pack their entire car of things into a single moving bin. Aaliyah denied her mother's offer to get a second bin. She saw another family wheel past her with a bin as full as theirs with items still sticking out of their trunk.

Aaliyah began to push the bin to the line Ally previously indicated. The three of them stood in line at the dorm. A scorching, eighty-five-degree sun was beaming down on Aaliyah, causing her to sweat. "Great, I'm gonna have sweat stains on the first day of meeting my roommate!"

"You'll be *fine*. She'll see you in much less and much worse." Her mother chuckled. Aaliyah stared at her mom to let her know her joke did not comfort her.

Aaliyah's mom placed her hand in Aaliyah's. "Listen. Don't expect to be best friends; just respect each other's spaces and you'll be fine." Tina pulled Aaliyah's head down to the crevice of her neck. Aaliyah bent down to her mother's five-foot-seven build. She whispered in her ear, "Plus, it may force you to explore and find a lil' boyfriend." Aaliyah could already see her smirk, as if she was the one checking in to a college dorm.

While they waited to be checked in, Aaliyah checked her phone. She was desperate to be comforted by a message from somebody at home. There was one.

> Damien D$: Hey, good luck up there. You'll be fine. I taught you to be smart in the streets, but you got the rest covered lol. Good luck.

Ty pushed Aaliyah's elbow forward, indicating she was next. A White girl with brown hair and green eyes smiled at them. "Hi, my name is Ashley, and I will be checking you in today. What is your first and last name?"

"Aaliyah Harris."

"Oh wow! I'll be your RA for the year. My partner in crime slash other RA is Jayden, but he's on the fourth floor helping everybody move in! I'm so excited to share the school year with you, Aaliyah!"

"Thanks... So do I get my key now? Or—"

"Of course! I just need to put a visitor sticker on your company and you three will be good to go!"

It seemed like every sentence she said ended with a chipper smile and an exclamation point. Aaliyah bent down to be eye level with Ty. She straightened out his shirt and put the orange sticker that said "VISITOR" in black bold letters on his chest.

"Okay, I have mine 'Liyah. Let's go." Tina politely smiled at Ashley and lead the way to the elevator line.

"Sorry!" Aaliyah heard Ty say a few steps behind.

A six foot, balding man with a peppered beard was smiling down at Ty. "That's okay, sport! You just gotta watch where you're going!" The man chuckled at his humor.

Aaliyah briskly walked over and grabbed Ty's hand. She gently forced him slightly behind her body. Ty's face scrunched at the joke he didn't follow.

"My apologies, sir." Aaliyah gave a deepened smile, showing her dimple on her left cheek.

Tina followed, "You take your eye off of them for one second, you'll lose 'em!" A chorus of laughter came and fell again.

"Well, y'all have a happy move-in day!" The man saluted the three and joined his family who were politely smiling behind him during the short interaction.

The elevator doors opened. Aaliyah shoved the bin in the elevator. Ty went on his heels and leaped into the elevator, his small force causing the elevator to shake. Aaliyah directed Ty to press four, and they jolted up. The family's silence in the elevator was deafening as Aaliyah tuned out the creaking. Her breathing became shallow, and her head became light. "Floor three."

Ty stood on his tippy toes to peer inside the moving bin. "Mom—"

Tina rubbed her thumb across the back of Aaliyah's clenched fists. "It'll be fine." Her voice soothed Aaliyah's sudden nerves.

"Floor four."

The doors opened. Ty repeated out loud, "four-sixteen, four-sixteen, four-sixteen," until they reached the door that had countless moving boxes and bubble wrap blocking the hallway. Tina stretched her neck to whisper in Aaliyah's ear, "They should be considerate enough to move their stuff out of the way though." She poked her lips out.

"Oh my goodness! I'm so sorry! Look at us! Blocking the entrance! Lemme clear that for ya," A heavy-set White man with a white beard, glasses, and a Giants baseball cap rapidly began removing the obstacle course in the Harris's way.

Aaliyah's mom waved his comment off, "Oh, don't you worry about that! If you would like, we can go to the bookstore and come back when you're all about done."

Aaliyah smirked at her mother's sudden switch up.

"That would be great. Thank you so much. I'm Chris, Chris Smith." He stuck out his hand and gave each of them a firm handshake, even Ty. Mr. Smith smiled at Ty's giggle from his body jolting around during their handshake. "My daughter Charlie is in this mess somewhere."

A pale, five-foot-nine girl with long legs and brown hair came bounding out of the room with opened skinny arms as she charged toward Aaliyah. "Aaliyah! I cannot tell you how excited I am. Just you and me in this room. We can color coordinate and add decorations. I brought nail polish so if you ever wanna borrow any, just let me know." Charlie spoke so fast she took a gasp of air when she was done.

Aaliyah glanced at her bare nails that she had only painted for prom.

"Oops! Look at me just rambling. Come in here and look at the view!" Charlie grabbed Aaliyah's forearm and pulled her into their twelve-by-nineteen-foot dormitory. Aaliyah stared at the view of Stanford City.

The clouds engulfed the sky as city life buzzed underneath them. Pine trees rooted into every barrier on the sidewalks. Aaliyah had never seen roads without a single pothole.

Aaliyah wanted to continue her gaze, but Charlie cut in, "My dad and I have been here since twelve, and it's two-thirty now. We'll get out of your hair. I need to go buy a laptop, and once you're settled, all five of us can go have lunch. Sound good?"

"Uh, yeah—"

Charlie squealed, "I'm so excited! Here's my number just in case you need to reach me at all today." Charlie handed Aaliyah a folded lavender sticky note she had ready in her pocket. Aaliyah unfolded the note to see "CHARLIE SMITH" in beautiful cursive letters. Her number was written with an area code Aaliyah did not recognize. There were hearts and smiley faces surrounding her bolded name.

She's almost as chipper as the girls checking in students, Aaliyah thought. The Smiths waved before they went out the door.

Aaliyah looked at her mom, eyes wide.

Her mother chuckled, "Time to start unpacking."

* * *

The three finished unpacking after a couple hours. They decided to explore the campus before meeting with the Smiths for lunch. Aaliyah texted Charlie the updated plan.

Charlie Smith: "Great! We're gonna finish unpacking the car. See you in an hour! So excited, roomie!"

Aaliyah stood in front of a pine tree surrounded by cement seating. "Hop on, Ty."

Ty jumped onto the seating and placed his skinny arms around her neck. They both took off, reenacting a cowboy and horse act. The game consisted of Ty telling her to "giddy up!" and controlling her shoulders to indicate which direction he desired to go.

"Don't go far, you two!" Their mother shouted as the two made distance between them.

"Okay!" they said in unison. Aaliyah placed her cheek on Ty's arm, grateful he was with her.

Ty steered Aaliyah's shoulders to the left. She galloped straight into the courtyard. Floods of families and students of a wide range of demographics were conversing with students in red shirts at different booths.

Aaliyah looked down at her outfit, suddenly self-conscious. She accounted for her baby blue and white tie-dye Champion tank top, cargo pants, and two-year-old white Air Forces that she took great care of.

"Hop down, buddy."

Ty slid off her back and wandered to the right.

"Ty, wait!"

Ty charged at a cornhole station set up next to a booth with a "Black Community Center" sign.

Ty had already thrown a beanbag by the time Aaliyah caught up with him. She wrapped her hand around his bicep until her fingertips touched. "You can't run off like that!" she hissed.

"But I'm glad he did."

Aaliyah dropped Ty's arm at the sound of the stranger's voice behind her. She turned to see a handsome, six-foot-one Black boy smiling back at her. He wore a light-gray beanie, short enough to reveal his pierced ears. She saw his waves peeking out from beneath his beanie. His dark brown eyes were staring into hers.

Aaliyah coughed to make sure her throat wasn't too dry to speak. "Hi, I'm Aaliyah," She tore her eyes away from his before she fell in a trance again, "and this is Ty."

"Nice to meet you both. I'm Jeremiah. I'm the Black Community Service Center's Cultural Chair. Are you two here for move-in day?"

"Yeah. We were going to the bookstore, but Ty here had other plans. My mom's around here somewhere."

Aaliyah looked around for her mom.

Jeremiah gave her a warm smile in return, "I think your mom is catching up to you." He directed his chin behind Aaliyah.

"There you two are! You're lucky I saw your two brown behinds before I walked into the bookstore." Mrs. Harris glanced behind Aaliyah and her lips formed a smirky pout. "Excuse me for interrupting!"

Aaliyah directly faced her mother and flared her nostrils, knowing what her mother was about to do.

"I'm Tina Harris. This is my daughter Aaliyah, as it seems you already know." She raised her eyebrow before continuing. "What do you have set up over here?"

"Hi, Ms. Harris, it's nice to meet you. My name is Jeremiah." He followed her over to the corn hole station. "Today the Black Community Services Center set up cornhole. Basically, you're aiming for the furthest hole but if you score in any, you're a winner in my book." He flashed another smile and a gem on his tooth reflected in the sun. Mrs. Harris laughed and gestured for Ty to come play with her.

Aaliyah watched them in the shade of the booth. She took her attention away from her family and admired the beautifully designed posters that were draped on the side of the booth. One was a silhouette of a Black man with half of his body outlined in Kente cloth, and the other half wearing a student athlete headband with university gear on. Another poster featured a Black woman with her arms folded. A third poster had a young Black girl blindfolded in a cotton field. Standing behind the girl was a man whose silhouetted body held the imprint of the American flag.

"These are really well done," Aaliyah said.

"You right," replied Jeremiah.

Aaliyah squinted to read the artist's signature. "Who's J. A.?"

Jeremiah stared at the picture with Aaliyah. "A really talented artist."

After a moment of happy tension, they both turned their attention back to her family. Her mother was cheering as Ty laughed. "I set up trivia questions about Black history but those two seem like they're having so much fun, I don't want to interrupt."

"I can answer for them."

He snapped his head to Aaliyah, "Oh, word?"

"Yup," she challenged with a smirk.

He reached in his pockets and pulled out several pastel-colored notecards. He began, "Who was Fred Hampton and how did he die?"

Aaliyah's smirk dropped, "Fred Hampton was a revolutionary part of the Black Panther Party. He was convicted of several petty crimes which sent him to jail in order to prevent him from uniting the other Black justice organizations. The government killed him."

Jeremiah nodded his head, stunned, and flipped a notecard. "Name three Black women who were victims of police brutality that still have not received justice today."

She looked up to see Jeremiah staring adamantly at her. She looked him in his eyes, "Sandra Bland. Aura Rosser. Michelle Cusseaux. Janisha Fonville. Tanisha Anderson."

Jeremiah flipped to the next card, "Who—"

"But that question is wrong."

"What?"

"You said name three Black women that were victims of police brutality who still have 'not obtained justice today,'"

Aaliyah put the last phrase in air quotes. "There is no verdict, settlement, or leave of absence that can bring back the life unjustly lost. My sister always says, 'Justice is a phrase fed to the mouths of those who are stripped of hope by the same people feeding us the facade of a justice system.'"

Aaliyah's phone pinged with a text. She brought it out of her pocket.

Charlie: "Hey girlie! My dad and I will be heading to lunch in about an hour. Is that okay?"

"Ma! Ty! Come on!" They shuffled over from their fun.

"I'm sorry but I have to go meet up with my roommate and finish…"

"Moving in."

"Yeah, see you around."

Aaliyah's mom pinched her elbow when they were out of Jeremiah's sight. "If you weren't Black, you would be blushing."

Tina giggled like a schoolgirl as she grabbed Ty's hand, leading the three to the bookstore. Aaliyah rolled her eyes behind her mother's back, knowing she was probably telling the truth.

Aaliyah walked into the bookstore and was immediately hit with a gust of cool air. She breathed in the comforting scent of books and smiled at the pitter-patter of feet walking on the open wooden floors. Aaliyah's mother briskly walked toward the Stanford gear section. She began to take clothing items off the rack and hold them out. She cut her eyes from Aaliyah's face, back to the shirt, back to her face and put it back. Tina repeated the same process for four other clothing items before Aaliyah became irritated.

"Mom!"

"What, girl! I'm trying to get you some gear before you're college-student broke and can't get it yourself."

Aaliyah pursed her lips together, knowing her mother was right. Aaliyah looked around for Ty, but he was not in her vicinity.

"Ma, *where's* Ty?" Aaliyah instantly began to panic. Her breathing became labored and her only thought was to find her little brother.

Aaliyah stepped out of the clothing section and scanned the bookstore. She saw the upstairs had a comic book section in their library. Aaliyah bounded up the steps, taking two at a time. She was out of breath when she saw Ty say, "Oo!" and pick up another comic book.

"Ty!"

He looked up at Aaliyah with fearful eyes once he registered the worry in his sister's face.

"*Why* would you leave Mom and I like that?"

Aaliyah pulled out her phone and texted her mother that she had found him. Shortly after sending the text, Aaliyah was startled by a booming voice.

"Excuse me. Is this your company?"

Aaliyah placed her arm around Ty's shoulder. "Yes."

"Well, we do not allow minors to wander around our store for safety precautions."

Aaliyah's mother came from behind the security guard officer whose hand was on his belt that was equipped with a taser, baton, and another device Aaliyah was unfamiliar with.

Aaliyah's mother stepped forward, "Well, we have him now. Thank you, officer." Aaliyah looked at her mom. She was staring intently at the officer, challenging him to do anything further. Both her feet were planted on the glistening wooden floor, and she blinked once.

The officer eased his hands off his belt and walked away without another word.

Aaliyah's mom placed her hand on both her children's backs and guided them to a dimly lit corner.

"Don't you *ever, ever,* walk away without telling us, do you understand me?" she loudly whispered at Ty.

He nodded his head while looking at the ground.

"Look at me!" she demanded. Ty's head snapped up. "That could have been dangerous. We are not at home where you can go where you please. You have to be responsible, young man."

I guess that means me too, Aaliyah thought.

Aaliyah's mom straightened out Ty's crinkled shirt and fixed his collar on his red and blue striped button-down shirt. She gave him a soft kiss on his forehead and told him to go pick out a comic book to bring back to Damien.

Ty rushed back over to the section like nothing happened.

Aaliyah and her mother stood, watching him from a few feet away. "The innocence of a child." Tina scoffed. "Sometimes you find yourself yelling because you want to instill your fear into them. So they can be more careful—more aware."

Aaliyah knew her mother shared her thoughts out loud at times.

Ty ran up to the both of them and presented the comic book he picked out. "Look! Me and Damien have been looking for this for forever!"

"Great!" Aaliyah's mom picked the book out of his small hand, "Let's go get *Black Panther: The Sound and the Fury* then."

"Are you *serious*? You would think by the time we've had our country's first Black president, we would have progressed past racially profiling *adorable* Black children," Charlie said, astonished by the story. Aaliyah nudged her mother's leg under the table, their knowing sign that discretely asked her mother whether she could "go in." Her mother nodded into her sip of iced tea.

Aaliyah intertwined her fingers and leaned across the table. "That's the thing; a Black president doesn't erase years of racism this country was built upon. Every institution was built on the backs of slaves in order to establish and maintain the economy we have today. *Adorable* Black children will no longer be racially profiled if we dismantle, abolish, and rebuild influential institutions. A diverse community must be involved in the reconstruction." Aaliyah deadpanned her roommate, perfecting her response after years of rebutting adults' opinions. She looked at Charlie, challenging her for a response.

"And *that* is why I will be majoring in Political Science. I want to help. I need to educate myself in order to become a better ally," Charlie gave Aaliyah a shy smile.

Aaliyah eased up. "What's your major, Aaliyah? If you've decided on one, of course," Mr. Smith inquired.

"Liberal Studies with a minor in Creative Writing. I'm really into poetry; it's a passion of mine."

"Why not major in English then?"

"Other fields need me more. The Black community needs me more," Aaliyah said quietly.

"Well, when I get to college, I'm going to major in fire-fighting!" The table laughed at Ty's comment.

* * *

Mr. Smith exchanged numbers with Aaliyah's mother so they could keep in touch for the girls' needs.

Aaliyah's mother's tears were already brimming as she barked picture orders to Ty, Charlie, and Aaliyah. Aaliyah thought she took over two hundred pictures in the span of seven minutes. The banner read, "WELCOME TO BELL-POINT" with the tiger mascot to the right. Aaliyah took a mental image of the sign—another visual accomplishment aside from her high school diploma.

The day of her high school graduation, her family arrived with balloons, bouquets of flowers, and horns that had the entire football stadium's ears ringing. When they returned to their block, the energy rang of Black pride and love. Aaliyah snapped out of her flashback as the camera clicked again.

"Okay, we need to hit the road, baby. I have work in the morning," Aaliyah's mother said with a steady voice and tears.

"Bye, Aaliyah, I'll miss you." Ty ran into Aaliyah's arms. She picked him up and spun him around.

"Bye, Ty, I'll miss you more. Make sure you bother Damien while I'm gone. Eat his favorite cereal for me." They both laughed and she put him down. He ran over to their mom who was a few feet away taking a video of the siblings' farewell.

"Come on, Momma, this will be one moment you can't film." Aaliyah gave her mother a tight hug. They both stood there for a minute, the silence louder than any words. After both sniffled, they pulled apart.

Her mother looked in her eyes, "I'm not worried about you. You'll find your way—you always do. You're the embodiment of resilience, and I love you."

"Call me when you get home," Aaliyah croaked out. The lump in her throat dared her to say another word. She patted the back of the Corolla as the two got in. Ty's head popped up from the backseat. He waved until they could no longer see each other.

Aaliyah sat on the curb, loneliness filling her. There was a tap on her shoulder. She had forgotten about Charlie. She turned around to see Charlie's pale face streaked with red lines accompanied by red, puffy eyes. Her face was incredibly red, as if she had fell asleep during a tan.

"Yes, I look like this every time I cry." Charlie gave a small laugh as she sat down on the curb.

Aaliyah gave a low-energy laugh at her comment. They sat there for a couple minutes in comfortable silence. Aaliyah decided to make the first move.

"You wanna finish unpacking?" She immediately became hesitant of her offer, wondering if Charlie felt as alone as she did.

Charlie's face lit up, "Yes, yes I would." Charlie hopped up, lending Aaliyah a hand. Aaliyah grabbed it and they fell into the same step on their way back to their dorm.

NOBODY TELLS YOU: HAPPY FIRST DAY

———

Aaliyah plopped in the chair to tie her shoes. Charlie was beside her throwing a couple notebooks in her bag.

Aaliyah looked behind Charlie's messy bun and saw "10:50 a.m." flashing above her tall stature.

"Is that the time?" Aaliyah shot up from her chair and began throwing things in her backpack. "Margaret Jacks Hall is a twelve-minute walk and I wanted to get breakfast. Guess that's out. Come on!" They both scrambled to grab backpacks, chargers, keys, and went out the door.

"I'll lock it; press the elevator button!"

Aaliyah sprinted down the hallway to bang on the button. She sighed as the elevator creeped to two different floors before reaching the fourth. Charlie was at the door by the time it opened.

They looked at each other in the elevator. Charlie's messy red hair remained in the bun from last night. Aaliyah was still untwisting her hair but they both laughed. Charlie nudged Aaliyah's arm, "Hey, happy first day, roomie."

Aaliyah and Charlie took advantage of their long legs and strode to Margaret Jacks Hall. They arrived with one minute left to sprint up two flights of stairs. Aaliyah yanked on the handle and ripped open the door. She was met with what seemed like a thousand eyes. They entered in the wrong door and were standing at the front of the lecture hall. Suddenly, Aaliyah was conscious of her hand-me-down outfit and three-year-old backpack.

Aaliyah looked to see the professor standing a few inches to her right. Aaliyah's embarrassment subsided as she smiled at her Black, female professor. Her professor smiled back.

Aaliyah fell into thought as she followed Charlie up the steps, allowing her to choose where they sat for their first class. Charlie set her backpack on the ground gently as the professor began speaking. "Good afternoon, class. We'll wait a couple more minutes for the folks still finding their way around campus."

The voices in the lecture hall increased, but Aaliyah blankly stared at the humming projector.

Wow, she's the first Black person I've seen at campus besides—

"Is somebody sitting here?"

Aaliyah's thought was cut off by Jeremiah hovering over her with a smirk. Aaliyah's mouth slightly dropped.

Charlie leaned across Aaliyah, removing Aaliyah's backpack from the seat Jeremiah was indicating, "Nope!"

Aaliyah snapped her head to Charlie and bucked her eyes.

Charlie smirked back at her, "What, he's cute."

Aaliyah turned to pay attention to the professor and felt Jeremiah's eyes on her.

"Alright!"

The room of thirty students quieted down.

The professor eased her posture and leaned on the table, "Good morning class, my name is Dr. Robinson and I teach the Writing and Rhetoric Class with a focus in poetry. I have a degree in English, Sociology, and received my master's in Public Relations. My passions include…"

Aaliyah's focus averted to a young girl coming through the side door out of breath. She scanned the classroom, ignoring the eyes that were staring at her, and found her target. She smiled and waved at Jeremiah. Aaliyah looked at Jeremiah with furrowed eyebrows. He smiled and waved back, pointing at the seat to his right. He moved his backpack when she found her way down their aisle.

Aaliyah turned to Charlie to express her dismay but found her roommate occupied as well. She was talking to the boy to her left. He had dirty blonde shaggy hair, muscular calves revealed by his khaki shorts, and a pair of Old Skool Vans.

Aaliyah, frustrated, turned to Dr. Robinson.

"…Become a better visionary of the future. In my class, we will break down your Western culture bias and envision a more inclusive future. We will discuss current events, social institutions, racial tensions, worldly issues, and so on. In order to be successful in my class I need effort and an open attitude."

As Dr. Robinson continued, Aaliyah studied her. She was a confident, educated intellectual. She was wearing a royal blue pantsuit and wore it well. She spoke confidently, rhythmic.

Aaliyah snapped out of her trance once Dr. Robinson asked, "Can anybody name a few poets?"

The classroom fell silent. Heads turned to see which student was brave enough to answer the simple inquiry.

"Porsha Olayiwola, Langston Hughes, Maya Angelou, Crystal Valentine," Aaliyah spoke up. She did not bother raising her hand. She was confident in her answer.

"Thank you…" the professor squinted her eyes at Aaliyah.

"Aaliyah," she confidently responded.

"Aaliyah."

"Now class, I understand this class will be challenging at times…"

"She knows poets too?"

Jeremiah nudged Aaliyah with his shoulder without taking his attention away from their professor.

Aaliyah gave him a side smile as she shyly looked at the ground.

"Alright, partner up. Meet somebody new, introduce yourself, and discuss with your new peer why you chose this class."

Aaliyah's stomach turned. She looked to her left to find Charlie giving her a pouty face while pointing at the shaggy-haired boy. Aaliyah grunted to herself. She turned to Jeremiah in hopes the other girl had found somebody new like the professor instructed. They both smiled at her and waved her over.

Aaliyah scooted her rolling desk-chair toward the two. "Hi," Aaliyah said warmly.

"Good morning, Ms. Harris. I should have known you would be in sophomore rhetoric and writing with yo' smart ass." Jeremiah leaned back causing his chair to creak.

"Yeah. I took AP Lang in high school." Aaliyah attempted to alter her laugh into a cute giggle but ended up snorting.

Jeremiah's friend looked between the two with a confused expression. She shrugged and offered her hand to Aaliyah, "Hi, I'm Kiley."

Jeremiah quickly sat back up, "Oh, my bad! Aaliyah, Kiley. Kiley, Aaliyah. Aye," he tapped the top of Kiley's hand, "tell her about the event tonight."

"Oh yeah, girl! You should come to the BCC tonight!"

Aaliyah failed to shield her confused expression.

Kiley waved off her confusion. "Black Community Services Center," she clarified.

"Tonight is the welcome-back-to-school slash welcome-to-school event. It allows new students to be welcomed into the Black community at school. While a small population, we are loved and supported!" Kiley reached in her backpack and opened a folder that read Bellpoint University in green bold letters. She handed Aaliyah a flyer.

"Okay! Would any of you like to share what you and your partners discussed?"

The students fell quiet again, the fear of their first interactions in class engulfing the room.

"Okay, no worries. You all will warm up to me." Dr. Robinson gave the class another bright smile. She went back to her projector and the class watched her pull up the class roster.

"I usually have to use this the first week since my students get shy on me." She scrolled down to the option "random generator" and pressed select. The class seemed to hold their breath until a wave of exhales flooded the room as one name flashed on the screen.

"Where is Jeremiah Anderson?"

Jeremiah coolly lifted his hand, holding two relaxed fingers in the air. "My group and I discussed that we picked your class because you had five stars on Rate My Professors."

A bubble of laughter overcame the room. Dr. Robinson joined the laughter, "Yes, I do happen to have a great reputation on campus. I was awarded the Outstanding Faculty Award for the last five years." Dr. Robinson popped her collar. This resulted in a rupture of laughs and whoops from the class—except Aaliyah. The energy in the room shifted. Students began to relax in their seats yet attentiveness visibly increased.

Kiley leaned toward Aaliyah, "She seems like she's gonna be cool."

Aaliyah turned to face Kiley and vigorously nodded her head.

"Now that you all have introduced yourselves, I want you to discuss a topic you'd like to explore while taking this course."

Aaliyah turned to face her group to find Jeremiah doodling on the back of the flyer Kiley had handed her earlier.

Kiley eagerly leaned toward the group. "Y'all, I ain't never had a Black woman professor before. This already my favorite class."

Aaliyah's eyebrows furrowed, "You said *never*?" Aaliyah whispered in worry.

Kiley tilted her head to the side and placed her hand on top of Aaliyah's, "No, girl. You probably won't find many Black professors, let alone Black women, outside of the African and African American Studies Department."

Jeremiah sighed loudly and rolled his eyes. "It's bullshit."

Kiley perked up, "But hey! If you come tonight, you'll be able to meet *many* Black professors."

Aaliyah slouched in her chair, reminiscing on every Black teacher she had back home.

"Okay class! By this time, you should have discussed your fears for this upcoming year. I want you to channel that for your *only* assignment in my class."

Class murmurings of the words, "only assignment," held a positive buzz floating throughout the lecture hall.

"Yes, it is the only assignment you will do in my class. I want each of you to complete a creative assignment by the end of the year. Whether that be through a spoken word performance, a short film, or a creative writing piece about a topic that resonates with you. I want your piece to inflict sympathy, pain, struggle, and passion. Now look to your left, look to your right. Whoever your partner or group is, you will be paired for this project."

Grumbles and moans erupted from all thirty students. The dreaded group project was upon them on the first class.

"Save the grumbling for your mommas! You have to learn to work with others in the workplace. Trust me, I'm helping y'all out!"

The clock changed from 11:49 a.m. to 11:50 a.m., and a chorus of zipped backpacks and increased chatter rose. Every student began to leave.

"I'll give you all more details about the group project next week. Go out and change the world!"

Aaliyah was slow gathering her stuff. She looked up from her backpack to see Jeremiah and Kiley patiently waiting for her while chatting. Charlie was next to them, entertained by the drawstring on her pants.

"You both can go ahead; my roommate and I are going to get some lunch before our next class," said Aaliyah.

Jeremiah hesitated but Kiley began walking toward the exit. She swiftly turned around and began walking backward. "Bye Aaliyah, see you tonight." She flashed a smile and Aaliyah admired how pretty she was.

She was dressed in a light-wash denim corset, paired with eggshell khaki pants. She complimented her outfit with a medium-wash denim bucket hat. Her brown curls spilled out from underneath the hat and Aaliyah noticed the blonde streaks in the sunlight. She was petite but her Air Force 1s made her stand a couple inches taller.

She walked out of the room with Jeremiah closely behind her.

Aaliyah scanned the room and became embarrassed that her and Charlie were the only ones left as Dr. Robinson packed her briefcase.

Aaliyah threw the rest of her materials in her backpack, desperate to leave the classroom. Charlie absentmindedly tied and untied her drawstring. Aaliyah broke her out of her trance, "Come on, Charlie. Let's go. I want to grab something to eat before my Statistics class at twelve."

Aaliyah opened the door. Charlie smiled at Dr. Robinson who watched them leave. "Bye professor, see you Thursday."

Aaliyah gave Dr. Robinson a faint smile. Charlie walked through the door and Aaliyah turned to follow.

"Ms. Harris."

Aaliyah's foot stopped the closing door. She poked her head in the classroom to find Dr. Robinson looking at her with the kindest smirk she had ever seen. "I look forward to your project."

Shocked, Aaliyah responded to the professor's comment with a breathy laugh. She stepped out of the room, the bright sunlight causing her to squint.

"Where do you wanna go eat?"

Before Aaliyah could answer, Charlie continued, "Because I've heard of some good places but the cute boy I was talking to in class today, *Grayson*..." she swooned.

Aaliyah took out her water bottle from the side of her backpack and tuned Charlie out. As she yanked her water bottle out of the sleeve, the flyer Kylie gave her earlier fell out. Without missing a breath, Charlie scooped her long arms down and picked up the flyer. She handed it to Aaliyah without glancing at it or stopping her story.

Aaliyah allowed Charlie to lead them to whichever food option she preferred while Aaliyah analyzed the flyer's intricate details. The lettering was all in maroon, forest green, and gold. The words "The Black Community Center presents—Welcome Home!" appeared in bold, surrounded by emoticons of Black women and men with afros and graduation caps.

"So, Coopera Cafe works?"

Aaliyah nodded.

Charlie clapped cheerily.

* * *

Aaliyah walked out of her second class of the day, drained. Luckily, the building was down the path from her dorm. She walked through the double doors and flashed her ID card. The young boy working at the front desk didn't even glance at her. Aaliyah waited for the elevators to creak down to the lobby. Four students walked out and a couple of them were in a rush as they began sprinting as soon as the elevator doors opened. Aaliyah laughed to herself as she rode in an empty elevator. She reached her room to find it empty as well.

You deserve a first day nap, Aaliyah thought as she eased her backpack off her shoulder.

Aaliyah jumped in her bed that was four feet off the ground and threw a blanket over herself. She opened one eye to set an alarm for 5:15 p.m., leaving her enough time to get ready for the event at 6 p.m.

* * *

After what felt like five minutes, Aaliyah's alarm was screeching. She slapped it and it fell into silence. Aaliyah turned to a fetal position to find Charlie sitting in her bed. Her wet hair let Aaliyah know she had just showered. Aaliyah sighed and slowly rolled out of bed. She glanced at her desk, grateful that she had placed her hair products out already. Next to her desk was the outfit she had draped over her closet door.

Aaliyah crouched under her desk and brought out her personal mirror. She placed it in front of her and began running Shea Moisture through her tightly coiled curls. Aaliyah placed a dime-sized amount of coconut oil in the palm of her hand. She began retwisting a few strands of hair that had flattened out from her slumber. Aaliyah tried to retwist another strand that was in the back of her head but couldn't see it. She turned her mirror to get a better angle but found Charlie's eyes no longer on her laptop. Her eyes roamed over the eight different products on Aaliyah's desk. Aaliyah continued to do her hair, seeing if Charlie would ask about them. After scanning the hair products once more, Charlie's eyes met Aaliyah's in the mirror, and she quickly averted her gaze back to her laptop.

Aaliyah took out her blow dryer from underneath her desk and ran her hands gently through her hair. She focused the heat on the pieces she retwisted then set the blow dryer down. She untwisted the pieces and they fell into place neatly. Aaliyah touched up her makeup and smiled at herself in the mirror.

"I'm going," Aaliyah slipped one leg through her jeans, "to a Black community event tonight."

Aaliyah couldn't see Charlie's face as she pulled over her graphic tee. Aaliyah paused, expecting Charlie to chime in.

As Aaliyah's head popped through her shirt, she saw Charlie intently listening to her.

"That sounds fun! Where is it?"

"The Black Community Center. But everybody calls it 'The Blackhouse.'"

Charlie yanked her covers off. "If I get ready fast, can I go?"

Charlie had already hopped off the bed and yanked open her closet.

Aaliyah's shoulders sank. "I don't think that would be a good idea…" Aaliyah's voice trailed off to a whisper.

Charlie's hands dropped from both of her closet doors. "Oh."

Aaliyah had never seen this look of confusion and despair on Charlie's face. "Yeah, because it's a Black event, hosted for Black community members. It's not that you're not welcome per say. It's more like—"

"It's not a space I should be inserting myself," Charlie finished.

"Yeah." Aaliyah nervously looked at her roommate.

"No, I get it." Charlie hopped back in her bed.

"Sorry…"

"No, no, have fun." Charlie gave Aaliyah a weak smile. Aaliyah's phone buzzed with a reminder that the event began in ten minutes.

"Well, it's a ten-minute walk. I'm gonna head out." Aaliyah turned to the door, grateful she had an excuse to leave the awkward tension.

"Okay, *bye*—" the door shut as Charlie said her farewell.

Aaliyah jogged down the hallway toward the elevator, not exactly sure what she was running from.

* * *

"She probably gave you that weird ass smile because she was embarrassed she even asked! As she should be!" Kiley shouted back in response to Aaliyah's recap.

Jeremiah was to the right of Aaliyah taking full advantage of the free food the event provided. "She right," Jeremiah commented through a mouthful of chicken wing.

"That's just like White people too! Always invading spaces that nobody asked them to be in." Kiley noticed Aaliyah's discomfort. "At least she checked herself."

Aaliyah shrugged, desperately wanting to move on.

The entire table jumped as a large hand slapped the top of Jeremiah's shoulder. Jeremiah almost choked on his chicken.

"Jeremiah! Young man! I see your artwork hung around the vicinity and I am impressed. I can tell you've been working on your craft. Keep it up, young man." The kind old man with gray dreads noticed the two young ladies watching their interaction. He kindly nodded in their direction, "Ladies," and dismissed himself.

Aaliyah turned to Jeremiah who was focused on another chicken wing. She put her finger between his mouth and the food. He looked at her as if she had grown another head.

"I wouldn't suggest that; he may eat your finger too," Kiley said nonchalantly while browsing her social media.

Aaliyah snatched her finger back, "*Your* artwork?"

Jeremiah smiled down at his plate.

"J. A.," Aaliyah said to herself.

"Jeremiah Anderson." He confirmed. "In the flesh." He threw his hands up.

Aaliyah abruptly stood up from her chair. "Come on. Show me the rest of your work."

Jeremiah looked down at his plate and began to pout.

"Boy, the way I watched you scarf down seven more pieces before she even got here. You're gonna grow a feather. Now go show her around." Kiley squinted her eyes at Jeremiah.

He squinted back while getting up and wiping his hands on a napkin. "Alright, come on, freshman."

Aaliyah laughed at the two's banter and let Jeremiah lead the way. Jeremiah brought her into the main hall where many students, administrators, and professors were conversing. Jeremiah smiled and waved at a few people as he weaved through the crowd. He checked behind him to ensure Aaliyah was following close behind.

He stopped near the entrance and pointed at an easel. It read, "WELCOME." Underneath the bolded letters was the Bellpoint tiger logo with the Black Power fist illuminated as its paw.

Aaliyah's eyebrows rose. She pointed to the easel and back to Jeremiah. He nodded with a proud smile. She was not able to fully admire the intricacy of the details before Jeremiah moved on.

She quickly fell behind him. Jeremiah stopped and stepped to the side as if he were revealing something behind a curtain. Aaliyah saw two more pieces that had ribbons on them. One piece caught Aaliyah's attention. It depicted two Black woman's facial features fading into one another. They had stark differences, but both had pain in their eyes. Aaliyah was captivated.

Aaliyah looked at Jeremiah. "This piece showcases the versatility of Black women while also showing different doesn't necessarily mean ugly as society paints Black woman to be. They're trendsetters, pioneers, and protectors all while remaining beautiful—"

Aaliyah's attention left the painting as Jeremiah passion-ately spoke about the meaning of his art.

"It's like being on this campus. You're surrounded by White people who keep trying to imitate Black culture."

Jeremiah hopped on the counter, moving his art to the side. "So, that's how Aaliyah feels about her 'new home.'"

Aaliyah dropped eye contact, embarrassed that she wasn't embracing the college spirit. "No, I—"

"It's okay, no need to explain. I want to show you something."

Jeremiah led Aaliyah around the corner. The secluded area was instantly quieter. Jeremiah looked up fascinated. Aaliyah followed suit. A seven-foot wall decorated with Kente fabric trimmed around the border was presented. Five rows of flyers were on the lower half of the wall. They ranged from "Black therapy options" to "Popular soul food places in Stan-ford." The upper half of the wall was blank.

Jeremiah answered what she was thinking, "This part everybody calls 'The Board.' Students come in, use a pen," he reached in a basket of pens that were next to the wall, "and write down suggestions for any events they would like to see hosted throughout the year."

Aaliyah nodded her head, already thinking of ideas.

Jeremiah continued, "But it doesn't have to be just event ideas. It can be suggestions of any kind. Kiley and I met because we collaborated on her idea to have a Black author come to school."

Aaliyah smiled at the authenticity of their friendship. Aaliyah reached in the basket and wrote the first suggestion of the school year on "The Board."

Jeremiah peeked over Aaliyah's shoulder and smiled. "Nice."

"My first day was fine, Momma."

"Did you ever talk to that boy again?" her mother responded intently.

Aaliyah debated her answer, "Actually... I have a class with him. He invited me to this event the Black community hosted at school. It was nice. I met some nice people that reminded me of home."

"Aw, baby, that's good! Look at you, taking advantage of your resources. And he invited you personally, did you say?" her mother pried.

Aaliyah began to regret telling her mother the truth. "Yes, Mom."

"Okay! Okay! I heard the attitude in your voice. I'll stop."

Aaliyah could practically hear her smiling. "But back to Charlie, what am I gonna do about *that*?" Aaliyah was glad her mother called on her walk back to her dorm. It gave her ample time to ask for advice.

"I told you. Don't go in expecting to be best friends. But if she asks questions, don't get frustrated. Be as open to explaining as she is to asking questions. She'll come around."

Aaliyah walked through the double doors and flashed her ID, wondering if anybody cared. "Okay. I'll be patient."

Aaliyah heard her dad in the distance, "That's my girl!"

Aaliyah laughed at her dad's poor eavesdropping skills. "Hi Dad."

She heard his voice clearly as he came closer to the phone, "Hi honeybee, hang in there!"

"Okay, well I'm getting on the elevator so the call may drop. I love you both and will talk to you later."

NOBODY TELLS YOU: NO MORE THROWING ROCKS

Aaliyah was awoken by a figure hovering over her, rapidly shaking her shoulders. Not her favorite way to wake up on a Saturday.

"Aaliyah! I'm sorry to wake you up, but I think you need to see this."

Aaliyah sat up to see the worry on Charlie's face. Charlie quietly slipped on her slides and Aaliyah followed suit. Charlie opened the door and lead Aaliyah to their floor's lounge. Four other students stood around the TV, listening intently, as it was on full volume.

A young female reporter stood beside a vandalized building. Firefighters were appearing and disappearing behind her.

"I am standing here at Bellpoint University, where at a reported 4 a.m., four unidentified individuals destroyed this school's Black Community Center. It is thought to have been an intentional attack made by students who attend the university."

Aaliyah sunk to the couch. One student saw Aaliyah's sunken shoulders and swatted his friend to move out of the way of her view. Aaliyah didn't want a clearer view. Suddenly, a sharp ringing formulated in her right ear. She closed the other ear with her finger, attempting to tune out the world. Aaliyah sat on the couch, looking at the ground. Tears threatened to escape, but a sudden wave of anger eroded every other emotion.

Aaliyah tore off the bonnet she was wearing. She clenched it in her fists and stormed back to her room, not caring if Charlie was behind her.

Aaliyah placed her key in the door and ripped it open. It flung against the wall, leaving a mark on the white paint. Charlie managed to slip through before the door shut.

"How are you feeling?" Charlie said above a whisper.

Aaliyah scoffed at the question.

"You don't have to talk about it. I'm sure it's frustrating—"

"*Frustrating*? Frustrating doesn't begin to describe it. It's frustrating and disappointing and hurtful and pitiful and—"

Aaliyah threw her bonnet across the room, and it fluttered gracefully in front of the door. Charlie stared at the bonnet until it hit the ground. "I'm literally just trying to be there for you! I'm your friend?"

"Well right now I want to be around friends that look like me. Ones that will understand what I'm going through without explanation."

Aaliyah didn't mean to attack Charlie, but she didn't regret what she said.

"Well, I don't get it. But I'm not going to add to your stress right now." Charlie got in her bed and faced the wall.

Aaliyah glanced at her before she walked toward the door. It looked like Charlie was about to cry which irritated Aaliyah further.

After the fourth second of silence, Aaliyah stated. "I'm leaving for a few." She slipped her slides back on and snatched up her keys.

As Aaliyah strode down the hallway, her phone buzzed. Charlie had sent her a message with an interview video from the news report. A young Hispanic man that Aaliyah recognized from her dorm floor spoke into the microphone, "Yeah, I was walking over after a workout, planning to do some homework and I saw it. Stunned. To see a safe space for African American students…*destroyed.* It's indescribable man. My heart goes out to the Black students on campus."

She continued down the hall as the news report played in the background like the buzz of an annoying bee. She couldn't decipher if she was grateful for the noise that was substituting her thoughts in her numb mind. When the elevator arrived at her floor the two girls in it stopped their conversation once Aaliyah stepped inside. Aaliyah avoided eye contact as they tried to give her a sorrowful look.

Aaliyah stepped out of the elevator. The stares felt like they were burning her cheeks. She walked down the air-conditioned hallway and goosebumps ran across her exposed arms. The need for a jacket disappeared as she thought about the BCC. Aaliyah stared at the ground. Before she stepped onto the crosswalk, a firetruck blew past her. She gasped and snapped her head in the direction it came from. Gravel transitioned into rubble and Aaliyah flicked the caution tape that was around what once was the Black Community Center. Aaliyah saw the firemen had hosed some black spray paint on the sidewalk.

Aaliyah looked around the premises to ensure nobody was around. Then she swiftly ducked around the caution tape and stood in the cold wind whistling through her thin pajamas. Aaliyah allowed impulse to take over her body and grabbed the first piece of debris she saw. She placed the piece of cement comfortably in her palm and threw it at the fallen building. She threw the rock with a scream bellowing into the quiet morning. Aaliyah felt pressure in her chest and sighed to prevent from letting out a sob.

A familiar ringtone came from Aaliyah's phone. She'd forgotten she had it in her left hand, gripping it so tightly the volume buttons on the side of her phone left indentations in her palm. She dipped back under the caution tape and answered the phone.

"Keisha," Aaliyah answered as if she had just finished a marathon.

"Hey, boo," Keisha responded softly.

There was a brief silence before Keisha continued.

"It's on national news, baby girl. How are you doing? Mom told us at dinner that you went there to study and see your friends a lot."

Aaliyah cracked, "It's just—it's a comfortable space for me. And they took it away…" Aaliyah crumbled to the sidewalk and began to cry. "They took it away," she whispered into the phone.

"I know—"

"Because they have the *power* to take it away! They can *fucking* vandalize property because they *know* they won't face consequences! And now it's gone."

"Aaliyah—" Keisha tried to cut in.

"I want them to face the same consequences they would make us face!"

"Preach!"

Aaliyah's shoulders relaxed as she laughed at Keisha's comment.

"Do you feel better?"

Aaliyah did not feel the same pressure on her chest. "Yeah, a little bit."

"I'm sure you had to get that off your chest. Are they offering free counseling or specific aid to Black students?"

"No. They haven't released a statement yet or anything. I'm sure whoever did it will be arrested."

There was a brief silence before Keisha responded. "I know it's hard right now, 'Liyah. But lean on others while you don't have this space. You know they won't attack anybody they aren't threatened by. But anyways, I love you. The whole family is thinking about you and sending you love too."

Aaliyah had a few aftershock hiccups from her cry and smiled into the phone. "Thank you for checking on me. I love y'all too." Aaliyah looked up from the ground as she heard footsteps approaching her. It was Dr. Robinson. "I have to go, Keisha. I'll talk to you later."

"Okay. Stay up! Stay—" Aaliyah hung up and mouthed "focused" before Dr. Robinson stood in front of her.

"Hey, Dr. Robinson," Aaliyah felt self-conscious in her strawberry-themed pajamas.

"Hi Aaliyah," Dr. Robinson sounded worn out. "I came by to see it too." She sounded as defeated as Aaliyah felt.

Dr. Robinson placed her fist underneath her chin. "I remember when I was recommended to be on the Board of Directors in order to build this beautiful center." She scoffed. "I won't lie, this news bent my spirit."

Aaliyah looked up at her professor. The fierce woman she met on her first day had been replaced by someone with slouched shoulders and worry lines running between her thin eyebrows. Her mourning look complemented her gray pantsuit. She stood to look at the ode to hate for another minute in silence.

Aaliyah's breath become labored as she felt the wave of defeat overtake her mind once again.

Dr. Robinson turned toward away from the destruction. She stared into the distance at the school's oldest building, standing tall and firm. She sat down next to her student and placed her hand gently on Aaliyah's knee.

After a few moments, Aaliyah forgot about her attire. She stared at the building Dr. Robinson was absentmindedly looking at. She thought about how Dr. Robinson must have been feeling worse than her—to see the rise and tragic fall of a building that was home to her students.

Aaliyah blurted out, "Aren't you mad?"

Dr. Robinson gave a tired smile. "I wish I could do the things they do to us to them. But I have to provide guidance to administration. I also have to remain hopeful around students or else we'll all be throwing rocks," she softly chuckled.

Aaliyah sat up straight and avoided eye contact with her professor. Dr. Robinson laughed and nudged Aaliyah. "It's absolutely fine to throw rocks and scream and cry." She looked Aaliyah in the eyes, "But it's not okay to give in to the hate. Nor is it okay to give up the fight. We choose how we will ensure a brighter future."

Aaliyah wanted to cry on her shoulder and express how much her words meant but the lump in her throat wouldn't allow it. "I'm gonna do more than throw rocks, Dr. Robinson. I promise." Aaliyah choked out.

Aaliyah slipped her feet firmly in her slides and stood up. "I'll start today!"

She began walking in the direction of her dorm, but Dr. Robinson's distinct voice cut through the cold air. "But I'll see you in class later?"

Aaliyah turned back to her favorite professor forgetting that it was Monday already. She gave her a smile and a vigorous nod. "Absolutely!"

Aaliyah pursed her lips and checked her phone to see how much time she had before class. Her clock showed 7:42 a.m. This time, she was more aware of oncoming traffic.

"Damn," she said under breath. An hour and fifteen minutes did not leave her enough time to devise a plan.

Aaliyah walked back to her dorm. Her eyes only focused on where her next long stride would be. She zipped past students that were groggily walking to their 8 a.m. classes. She tried to squeeze her thin frame past two group of boys talking about their fraternity duties. One boy took a step back and swung his metal water bottle in Aaliyah's abdomen. She gasped for a breath as she stumbled back from the impact. Her vision went blurry.

* * *

"Yeah, just stand right there." Damien placed both of his hands on Aaliyah's shoulders.

She looked questionably at the two largest pillows in the house taped around her stomach and back.

"Damien, why can't you do this with Dad," Aaliyah whined.

"Because Dad won't get home till eight, and I need to be at an art show by then," Damien fired back. "But I appreciate it," he added sweetly.

Aaliyah knew if he was showing appreciation, she wouldn't like what's coming next.

"Okay, bend your knees a little and try and stay in place."

Aaliyah did as she was told and scrunched her eyebrows at her older brother. He took two steps toward her and used all his momentum to plow in the middle of Aaliyah's stomach. She flew back on the floor as the pillow cushioned her intense drop. Aaliyah scrambled off the floor and ripped the tape from around her torso.

* * *

"My bad, I didn't see you behind me" A tall scrawny boy with beach blonde hair and a pointed nose snapped Aaliyah back into reality. He was standing next to the boy Charlie was gushing about. Chase? Grant? Aaliyah didn't care at the moment.

"Or maybe you could stop standing in the middle of the walkway," Aaliyah shot back. She straightened her shoulders, feeling confrontational.

The boy looked at Aaliyah for a second and turned back to his group. "Alright boys, let's move out of the walkway."

Aaliyah raised her eyebrow and continued her journey, trying to contain the internal celebration. She only got a few steps before she heard, "She was in *strawberry* pajamas, bro. You had that."

"I don't care, they're probably going through a tough time right now."

Aaliyah's shoulders sunk as she realized her self-proclaimed victory was an opponent surrender. She walked into her building, trying to avoid all interaction.

"Excuse me! I didn't see your ID!" said the same young man that hadn't checked the previous night.

Aaliyah yanked her lanyard out of her pocket. She tauntingly waved it in the boy's direction. "Here! Not like there's many Black people here anyway. You should recognize me by now." She stormed off before the stares from the few students in the lobby turned into more unwanted interaction. Aaliyah pressed the elevator button seven times before it arrived. She utilized the alone time to sort out her emotions. She couldn't go over her last outburst before the elevator arrived at her floor.

Aaliyah walked back to her dorm and saw her room was cracked open. She saw Charlie on the phone as she multi-tasked with organizing her backpack. Charlie's hair fluttered behind her back as Aaliyah swung the door open. Charlie gave her a shy, empathetic smile. Aaliyah returned a blank stare and opened her closet.

She threw on a white tee and a pair of sweatpants that her mom bought her at the bookstore. She slipped on her slides and sat in her desk chair. She placed her foot on the ground firmly to keep the chair from spinning. She glanced at her phone which was charging next to her—8:14 a.m. She saw a notification under the time from the university. She opened the email:

"Bellpoint Community,

Today, an act of violence was brought upon the Black Community Center—an act we do not stand with. Bellpoint University is an institution that does not stand for hate and violence, nor condone of such. Fortunately, we are in a community that is open to change in order to support students from every background. I am reminded of the words from Dr. Martin Luther King who, in his Nobel Peace Prize speech, said: "I believe that unarmed truth and unconditional love will have the final word in reality. This is why right, temporarily defeated, is stronger than evil triumphant." We cannot allow these acts of treacherous hate overshadow the commitment to hope and love that continues to prosper on this campus.

WHEN SUPPORT IS NEEDED

- **Counseling Services** located at the Jamacha Center. They are open from 8 a.m. to 2 p.m. Call (650) 555-0108 to make an appointment, as they fill up fast.
- Contact the Dean of Students, Katy Palmer, at (650)555-0125 to address personal student concerns.

MOVING FORWARD

Therefore, we are hosting an open forum for students to speak about the grievances of the recent event. The forum will be at the Impala Center on Wednesday at 6 p.m. We aim to amplify Black students during this discussion so we can improve as a university."

Aaliyah slid a college-ruled piece of paper from her desk organizer and pulled out her favorite pen. She clicked the pen a few times and titled the paper "Burn It Down," with a thick bold line underneath. Aaliyah used her other foot to refrain from shaking her leg, a nervous habit she had failed to break despite her mother's persistent asking. Aaliyah stared at the paper, tilting her head after a few moments to see if it would give her any ideas. Aaliyah scrambled to pull her phone off the charger and pull up the interview released that morning.

Aaliyah put her headphones on and played the video twice, pausing at the before and after pictures of the center. She paused the video and took a screenshot of the remains. Her stomach became queasier the closer she zoomed in on the photo.

A screeching alarm managed to make its way through Aaliyah's soundproof headphones.

"Come on. We gotta go to class. You coming?" Charlie asked. Concern was laced in her voice.

Aaliyah looked at herself in the mirror placed at the edge of her bed. Her hair was disheveled, and her ashy ankles peeked from beneath her sweatpants that were two inches too short. She yanked open her backpack, causing her zipper to fall off track, and pulled out some deodorant.

"Yeah, I'm ready."

NOBODY TELLS YOU: THERE ARE NEVER THREE STEPS

———

Aaliyah slammed her laptop closed after rereading the email. The student in front of her looked back but quickly turned around after being met with Aaliyah's stony look. Jeremiah sat down without Aaliyah acknowledging him. The tapping of her feet increased with her heartbeat. She waited for class to begin so it would distract her hostile thoughts.

"You saw the released statement?" Jeremiah said, observing her body language.

"Yeah. It's bullshit. Did you see the part titled, 'Moving Forward'? How are we going to 'Move Forward,'" Aaliyah mocked, "when we haven't even addressed the problem?" Aaliyah's voice rose. Students peered in Aaliyah's direction to see where the commotion was coming from.

"Nah, I didn't read it." Jeremiah leaned back in his seat. The bags underneath his eyes indicated he had a restless morning as well. His melancholy voice soothed Aaliyah for a reason she couldn't figure out.

"Why not?" she asked confused. She made sure to lower her tone to match his.

"A group of people came to campus last year promoting some anti-immigration laws. They claimed to be on the side of the law but, in reality, they were just spewing hate." Jeremiah unraveled his headphones and placed one in his ear as more students came flooding into the classroom cheerily.

She heard him say, "Uneducated motherfuckers," under his breath.

She looked at him questionably, "What does that have to do with this?"

He sighed heavily and paused his music, "They released a statement saying something that's probably along the same lines. 'We don't stand for this as a university. We must come together as a community and stand strong against hate.' If they were complacent about an issue that regards people that aren't even enrolled here, then they for sure won't do shit when it comes to students here." He cleared his throat and pulled his baseball cap further down his forehead. "I have no interest in seeing what they have to say."

Dr. Robinson stepped into the classroom. She was wearing a different pantsuit than earlier this morning and Aaliyah noticed she'd put more powder under her eyes to hide their sunken appearance. "Sorry I'm late, class." Dr. Robinson allowed her commanding voice to quiet down the room.

Once the room was silent, she continued, "I'm sure today is heavy for many of you." She placed her forefingers on the chair in front of her. "It is for me too. Today, I want us to take the first few minutes of class to have open dialogue about what we've seen and how we can progress. Who would like to start us off?"

The class looked around shyly wondering which brave person would raise their hand first. Dr. Robinson patiently waited with her students. A wave of swiveled heads turned to see whose pale hand was in the air. Aaliyah turned to her left to see Charlie's hand in the air. Charlie met Aaliyah's confused stare with a small smile.

Dr. Robinson nodded her head at Charlie. "Yes miss, can you please state your name for the class."

Charlie sat up straight, "Hello, my name is Charlie Smith. I would like to begin the conversation by saying what a despicably hateful crime this was. It is disheartening to see that African Americans have to deal with so much in society but also have to face the destruction of their space. They no longer have a center for resources or community."

Dr. Robinson gave Charlie a full smile. "Thank you for your input, Ms. Smith. Does anybody have a response to her comment, or another point they would like to add?"

A young man in the front row placed his elbow on the desk. He had jet-black hair slicked with a lot of gel, paired with a matching thick mustache.

Dr. Robinson looked down, "Is that a raised hand?"

He nodded, "Yes, it is, Professor. I would like to add that the intent of this destruction was malicious. Hate crimes against Black and Brown people in America have always baffled me. Assuming the criminals were White, what did they gain from it? They destroyed a safe space for Black people; now what?"

"Because they want to pose a threat when in reality they're scared."

The entire class turned to look at where the comment came from. They were met with an agitated Kiley.

"Sorry to interrupt you, but there's always a reason for these crimes. They stem from selfishness, hatred, but most of all, fear. White people oftentimes rationalize their racist behaviors by accusing Black or Brown people of being violent, when in reality, they're the most brutal of all. A basic history lesson will prove that."

"Then what's the excuse for Black-on-Black crime?" A young man in the third row added. His fists were balled up causing them to turn a paler shade of white than they already were.

Kiley pretended to cough, "Colonizer." The class tried to cover their chuckles. Kiley looked proud. The young man pursed his lips until they disappeared into his face.

Aaliyah scrunched her face as if she tasted something spoiled. She remembered the facts Keisha would bring home when she returned from her community college courses her junior year of high school.

Aaliyah spoke up, "Black-on-Black crime isn't a real thing. Black people are forced into ghettos and that environment results in violence, gangs, and poverty. If you educated yourself, you would know that Jewish people were placed in ghettos during World War II and the same result occurred. But you wouldn't know that from the suburban world."

Dr. Robinson cut in before the discussion unfolded, "While Ms. Harris is correct, let's remember to be respectful during this discussion. I would like this to be a safe, healing space during this time of emotional strain."

Aaliyah gave the boy who made the comment a squinted look, but he failed to make eye contact. Aaliyah looked to her left to see Charlie fully engaged.

"Dr. Robinson, may I add?"

Aaliyah snapped her head to Jeremiah who previously looked irritated at the beginning of this discussion.

Dr. Robinson gave a warm smile, "Of course, Mr. Anderson."

"I think this conversation is vital but it's disappointing that this is the only class I'm having this discussion in. In addition to that, you're my only professor of color and I don't think that's a coincidence."

The class fell back into silence. Dr. Robinson nodded her head. "I want us all to carry this conversation with us. Allow the different perspectives to cultivate your mind into being more aware of somebody that is not in relation to your own community. Strive to become better people for one another every day."

Dr. Robinson walked behind her desk to turn on the projector. The class broke off into quiet separate conversations. The room buzzed with voices. Aaliyah sat there in silence. She wondered if her English professor would address the vandalism. They were currently writing essays on Critical Race Theory. She thought about the only other Black student in that class.

Charlie turned to Aaliyah as Dr. Robinson was still getting prepared. "Hey, I'm gonna go to the bathroom real quick. I'll be back soon."

Aaliyah moved her long legs to the side so Charlie could squeeze through the narrow aisle. "Okay."

About five minutes into the lesson, Aaliyah's head fell back twice throughout the class from her falling asleep. Jeremiah discretely put his hand on her knee and shook it. That woke her up.

Damn, if I was the same complexion as Charlie, my cheeks would be red, she thought.

Aaliyah reached into her backpack and pulled out her phone. She double checked to make sure it was on silent. She pulled up the released statement to confirm the dean's name. She typed in "Katy Palmer, Bellpoint University."

A page uploaded on the university's website. Aaliyah clicked the link and was met with the Dean's credentials. She was a third-generation legacy at Bellpoint. She was involved in several organizations in her undergrad. After obtaining her bachelor's, she received a master's in public relations. After serving underneath the university's provost, she went back to receive her PhD. Shortly after, she was selected to be the Dean of Students at an astounding thirty-one.

Aaliyah slouched in her seat and bent her posture so she'd be hidden by the large boy in front of her. She placed a headphone in and rewatched the news tape. She wrote down the pieces of evidence the reporter announced.

"Four male individuals all wearing black. Drove a Land Rover Range Rover. One individual said to have handwritten markings on the side of his shoes. If you have additional evidence, you can contact Bellpoint University's police station."

Aaliyah accepted her fate of zoning out this class and decided to remain productive. She pulled out the same piece of notebook paper she had written on earlier in her room.

- "Assort the pictures you found in the video.
- Find a piece of evidence from the 'crime scene.'
- Contact Dean of Students, Katy Palmer."

Aaliyah checked her phone and noticed Charlie had been gone for a while. She looked to her left feeling a loss of energy when she saw the empty seat. Aaliyah scooted Charlie's backpack underneath her chair. As she bent down to move the backpack, she noticed Grayson excessively shaking his right leg. He saw Aaliyah looking at his leg and impulsively stomped on his right foot with his left. She noted the slight sweat forming around the rim of his forehead, causing his hair to lay flat.

Aaliyah kept an intense stare on Grayson when she felt a tap on her back.

"Sorry, I'm trying to get back to my seat," Charlie whispered, attempting not to interrupt Dr. Robinson.

Aaliyah released her tight grip on Charlie's backpack and repositioned herself back in her seat.

"What are you working on?" Jeremiah leaned in to whisper in Aaliyah's ear. He looked down at her paper and pointed to the title.

"Come with me after class," Aaliyah whispered back.

Twenty minutes dragged by. Aaliyah perked up at the chorus of students zipping their backpacks. She was still not used to bells no longer dismissing her.

"Alright class, I'll see you next week." Dr. Robinson's farewell was met with students erupting out of their seats. Aaliyah noticed how fatigued her professor was as she passed up her usual chipper goodbyes.

Jeremiah, Aaliyah, Charlie, and Grayson were the last few students to exit the building. "Bye, Dr. Robinson!" Jeremiah and Aaliyah said before shuffling out of the crowded doorway.

Aaliyah turned around to face Charlie. "Hey, I'm going to go with Jeremiah right now. We have to work on…a project… for, um, my other class."

Charlie tilted her head, "What class do you two have together besides this one?"

Jeremiah jumped in when he saw Aaliyah's eyes grow wide, "I'm helping her on her application for the BCC. She didn't want to tell anybody so she doesn't jinx it."

Aaliyah nodded vigorously.

Charlie clapped, "*Aw*! I'm so excited for you! You're totally going to get whatever position you apply for. I hope they begin reconstruction soon." Charlie shook her head.

She turned to Grayson, "Where are you headed?"

He shook his head and looked at the ground, "I'm supposed to meet up with my boys."

Charlie looked slightly disappointed and perked up as quickly as her face dropped. "No worries! Everybody's doing their own thing. I'm going to go spend this meal plan money. I'll see everybody later."

"Bye, Charlie!" Aaliyah called after her.

"Later, Charlie!" Jeremiah waved.

"I gotta go this way." Grayson nodded his head to the left and broke off to another pathway.

Aaliyah and Jeremiah lifted their hand as a farewell.

"Okay, let me see that." Jeremiah stuck his hand out. Aaliyah handed him her plan and picked up her pace.

He began reading it to himself, "Step one… Step two… Aaliyah, these steps aren't as easy as a one, two, three, victory! Hooray!"

Aaliyah glared at him without slowing down, "I know that. But I'm not throwing rocks anymore."

Jeremiah looked at her confused, "Is that some alternate version of kick rocks I don't know about?"

Aaliyah chuckled, "No but we're going to the BCC now to find some evidence that will help our case."

"*Our* case?" Jeremiah pointed his finger at his chest.

Aaliyah felt her eyes getting hot. "You're not gonna help me?" Her voice cracked.

Jeremiah couldn't deny her pleading eyes. "Yes, I'm gonna help you. But don't expect a huge victory. I told you what happened last year."

Aaliyah looped arms with him, "But they didn't pay tuition. We. Do." Her beaming smile was placed back on her face as they headed for the BCC again.

Jeremiah looked down at Aaliyah. He admired how hopeful she was no matter how much her persona would deny it.

The two arrived at what was once the BCC. Aaliyah took in where The Wall was, now in smithereens. She ducked under the tape.

"Aye, you can't do that! It's in the middle of the day; somebody's gonna see you!" Jeremiah warned as he remained behind the tape.

"I'll be quick. I feel like I need to find something." Aaliyah found herself in the middle of the tape. She closed her eyes and felt the heat of the living room. She saw the beautifully decorated welcome sign that propped open the heavy metal door. She saw Black mentors and students entering the building, excited to see each other. Aaliyah opened her eyes and held eye contact with Jeremiah, both mourning a home.

Disappointed, Aaliyah ran back toward Jeremiah. He pulled the caution tape down as she hopped over.

They both heard, "Shut the fuck up, Dawson!"

Jeremiah pulled Aaliyah behind a shrub. The shadow of the bush hid them from the oncoming voices.

"I told you, we're good. Not only are they not gonna catch us, but even if they do, my family's the top donor of this school. We're not going anywhere, brotha!"

Aaliyah leaned out from behind the shadows to see who was talking. The voice sounded familiar. She heard the footsteps come closer to their hiding spot. She hopped up and gestured for Jeremiah to follow.

"Yeah, I still don't know what I'm going to do for the final project," Aaliyah nonchalantly came from out of the shadows.

"Yeah, me neither," Jeremiah responded coolly.

Aaliyah almost ran into the ones who were talking until the familiar voice held a hand out to prevent the collision. "My bad." He was walking with the boy who had asked about Black-on-Black crime earlier in class—Dawson, apparently.

"You're good." Aaliyah made sure to scan his entire body. She looked to see who he was with. It was the same boy that she had bumped with her backpack—the same one Grayson shut down. The boys gave a quick glance to the two and proceeded toward the fraternity houses behind the Center.

"Hey!" Aaliyah couldn't stop herself. The two boys turned around. "You were the one in class asking about Black-on-Black crime, right?"

Dawson placed his left hand behind his neck, "Yeah, I just didn't know."

Aaliyah shook her head at his answer. Jeremiah placed his hand on Aaliyah's hip. "We'll see you next class, bruh."

The two parties turned the opposite direction but not before Aaliyah heard Dawson's friend say, "Who was that bitch?"

Your worst nightmare, she thought.

* * *

Jeremiah and Aaliyah made it back to the quad. Aaliyah wrote the description of the two boys on her notebook paper.

"Now what's next on your plan? Go to the Dean?" Jeremiah sat down on a bench.

Aaliyah plopped down next to him, "Yeah. It's only 12:20. Her office doesn't close till five."

Jeremiah sighed, "I have an appointment with my academic advisor at 12:45. I can't go with ya, kid."

Aaliyah hid her disappointment, "That's okay. You have other responsibilities. Go handle your business." She gave him a side hug. He wrapped his long arm around her shoulders and pulled her into his chest.

"Okay but know that you don't have to conquer the world in one day. You should rest, eat, replenish." He placed his hand on the back of her head, "I'll catch you later."

Aaliyah remained on the bench. She appreciated the slight breeze that flowed in the shade. Her stomach grumbled so loud a few students walking by looked up from their phones. She realized she had not eaten since waking up that morning.

"We choose how we will ensure a brighter future," Aaliyah mumbled to herself.

Aaliyah put her hand in her backpack and felt around until her fingers grazed plastic wrapper. She pulled out a two-week-old granola bar. The plastic rustled in the slight breeze. Aaliyah placed her hand on her stomach to monitor any more grumbles.

Aaliyah pulled her phone out from the same backpack pocket the granola bar was in. The page of Dean Katy Palmer popped up. She confirmed which building she was in. The Student Representation building, next to Dr. Robinson's class. Aaliyah slung her backpack over her shoulders and walked back in the direction of the building.

After a short walk, Aaliyah stood in front of the censored door. There was a building directory at the entrance.

"Katy Palmer, Floor 5." Aaliyah walked into the elevator that was to the right of the directory. The elevator creeped to a stop and three businessmen exited the elevator. All three men had slicked back hair, suits, and briefcases. One man gave a nod before Aaliyah stepped in and punched five.

Aaliyah pulled out her notebook paper from her back pocket. She flattened out the wrinkled edges. She took a deep breath once the elevator beeped at floor four. The elevator jolted to a stop at five and she plastered on a smile.

Aaliyah walked down the long corridor. She checked each door that was labeled with an office or name. Aaliyah stopped when she read "Students Service Center—Katy Palmer."

Aaliyah rubbed her sweaty palms on her sweatpants, careful to not damage her notebook paper. She walked up to a young woman with blonde hair pulled up into a sleek ponytail. She had on a blazer with what Aaliyah assumed to be paired with a pencil skirt. Aaliyah couldn't tell as her legs disappeared under the large, cherry, wooden desk.

"Hi! How may I help you?" she smiled at Aaliyah revealing perfect teeth under her pink lipstick.

"Hi, I'm here to meet with the Dean, Katy Palmer."

"Sure. What's your first and last name?" The young woman began typing on the computer illuminating her face.

"Aaliyah Harris." Aaliyah scanned the room as the assistant searched the computer. The room was vacant, and the only noise was the blasting AC. The wooden desk matched the coffee table that was to Aaliyah's right. On the table was a Bellpoint newspaper below a glass bowl of different-colored marbles. Behind the assistant was a large conference room. The room had tinted windows, but Aaliyah could see the conference desk. To the left of that was an office. Aaliyah couldn't make out what the label said on the door from her angle.

"I'm not seeing an Aaliyah Harris. I'm so sorry. What time was your appointment?" The young woman looked at Aaliyah concerned she had forgotten to schedule an appointment.

"I don't have an appointment." Aaliyah looked at her desk tag. "Tiffany."

Tiffany looked up from her computer, "Oh, Dr. Palmer only takes appointments. You'll have to come by another time."

Aaliyah took a moment to search for the released statement, "No. It says to come *here* if there are any personal concerns." Aaliyah flipped her phone to reveal the statement to Tiffany.

Tiffany scrunched her eyebrows and quickly went back to her fake smile. "*No,*" she responded with the same attitude Aaliyah previously gave. "It says to *contact* the Dean if there were any personal problems. It lists the number right there." Tiffany tapped on Aaliyah's screen. Aaliyah snatched her phone back.

"Tiffany, I need fourteen copies of the—" Dr. Palmer walked out of the office Aaliyah assumed was hers. She was in a pantsuit. Her white blouse underneath her blazer had ruffles on the chest. She was smaller than Aaliyah had imagined and had aged several years since taking the picture on her campus profile. Her nose looked pointy as well.

"Oh, hello." She greeted Aaliyah when she saw their vacant office had company.

"Hello Dr. Palmer. I came to see you." Aaliyah boldly stated.

"Dr. Palmer…" Tiffany stood from her chair. "I tried to tell this student that she must either contact your office through telephone or make a scheduled appointment."

"Well, can I schedule an appointment now?" She stated her question and held intense eye contact with Tiffany.

"No—"

"That's fine, Tiffany. I'll see her now." Dr. Palmer dropped a file of papers on Tiffany's desk.

She walked toward Aaliyah who was towering over her five-foot frame. Aaliyah noticed her quick glance at her ensemble. Aaliyah suddenly wanted to put socks on her exposed toes and ankles. She reminded herself of her purpose.

Dr. Palmer placed her hand in the center of Aaliyah's back. "My office is over here. I would be happy to talk to you today."

Aaliyah remained silent until Dr. Palmer was sitting in front of her. Aaliyah felt like she was at the principal's office or a parent-teacher conference. This time, it wouldn't be for good behavior.

"Good afternoon, Dean Palmer. My name is Aaliyah Harris—"

Dr. Palmer cut off the speech Aaliyah had practiced in her head. "Nice to meet you. What concerns did you come in with today?" She gave Aaliyah a warm, encouraging smile.

"I know who vandalized the Black Community Center." Aaliyah stated. She wanted to exude confidence, so she intertwined her hands and placed them flat on the desk.

The Dean's smile dropped. "Okay, honey, you can't come in here and make bold assumptions like that."

Aaliyah's face contorted into a cringe, "It's not an assumption. I have evidence."

Dr. Palmer's face became pale. "Okay." She held out her hands.

Aaliyah pulled out the now crumpled notebook paper. She placed it on the edge of the desk to quickly flatten the crinkles.

Dr. Palmer's gaze remained on the piece of paper, her sickly expression not changing.

Dean Palmer's face contorted into a sour cringe as she reexamined the evidence Aaliyah presented.

Aaliyah placed the paper in front of her, slipping it upside down so the Dean could read.

Aaliyah began, "First, the news report mentioned that the individuals were students that attend this university. So, today in class we were discussing the vandalism—"

"What class is this?" The Dean cut her off.

"Sociology 104 with Dr. Robinson…" Aaliyah gave her a confused look.

Dr. Palmer shook her mouse and began typing. Without looking back at Aaliyah, she said, "Continue."

"Okay… Well, the discussion was going well until one student decided to bring up 'Black-on-Black crime.' I had to dispute his irreverent comment and then after class, I saw him again! We heard him say—"

Dean Palmer stopped typing, "Who's we?"

Aaliyah stopped her ramble, "I mean I."

Dr. Palmer nodded with an eyebrow raised, "Continue."

"Okay, so I saw the boy when I went to the BCC after class and him and another friend said, and I quote, 'Shut the fuck up Dawson! I told you, we're good. Not only are they not gonna catch us but even if they do, my family's the top donor of this school. We're not going anywhere brotha!'" Aaliyah imitated their conversation.

Dean Palmer looked at Aaliyah after she placed her thin, wire-framed glasses over her slim noise. "Who said this exactly? What are their names?"

"The student who was told to 'shut up' is named Dawson. The second student, I'm not quite sure of his name but I can describe what he looks like," Aaliyah responded confidently.

Dr. Palmer pounded each letter on her keyboard. "No, that's okay. Continue."

Aaliyah frowned, "That's it."

Dean Palmer looked at Aaliyah over her glasses with her hands hovering over her keyboard, "That's it?"

Aaliyah nodded.

Dr. Palmer intertwined her fingers and leaned in toward Aaliyah. "Honey," she took off her glasses, "this is not enough evidence to find and question these students. This is all speculation." She waved her hand over Aaliyah's notebook paper.

Aaliyah leaned away from the Dean. "Jeremiah was right," she said to herself.

"Excuse me?" Dr. Palmer responded while gathering papers.

Aaliyah felt the anger rise, "So why did y'all release a statement saying to reach out for support if you're not going to even do that?"

"Sweetheart—"

"My name's Aaliyah," she responded coldly.

"Okay, Alayah—"

"Aaliyah. Like, *uh-lee-uh*," she enunciated. "With all those degrees," Aaliyah said under her breath.

Dr. Palmer pursed her lips, "Aaliyah. These options are still available, but we didn't mean trying to solve an entire vandal case on your own." She tried and failed to stifle a laugh. "Our campus authorities are on that as we speak."

"What are you going to do with the information I told you?" Aaliyah gestured toward the computer.

"I'll present it to the correct authorities, and they'll take it from there. We're doing everything in our power to make sure students on campus feel safe again." She gave Aaliyah a reassuring smile she had mastered.

"So we're done here?" Aaliyah asked, packing her things.

"Yup! Thank you for coming in!"

Aaliyah reached for her notebook paper, but Dr. Palmer's hand slammed on top of it, creasing it once more.

"But I'm going to need to keep this." She returned Aaliyah's cold stare until Aaliyah's hand released the paper.

Once her hand lifted, she painted on her smile, "I can turn this into campus police station so they have tangible evidence."

Aaliyah lifted from her seat feeling cold, and not from the AC. She pulled on the door handle, and it creaked open. "Thank you for being such a great help, Aaliyah! You can come back if you need anything else any time."

Aaliyah kept her back to the Dean, not acknowledging her statement. She walked past Tiffany in silence while Tiffany smirked at her defeat.

She walked down the long corridor with her head down.

NOBODY TELLS YOU:
FIGHT BACK

———

Aaliyah opened the fridge as if something new would appear since she'd checked an hour ago. The fridge was too small to fit any new items anyway. She crouched down to wipe the dusty fridge with a Lysol wipe. She thought about how her mother claimed she wouldn't keep up with her cleanliness once she was not under her supervision. Aaliyah laughed to herself. She pulled off a flyer from six weeks prior that read, "Black Community Center presents—Welcome Home!"

Aaliyah balled up the thick piece of paper and shot it in the trash can five feet away. "Kobe," she said when it landed in the trash can.

Charlie jiggled her keys in the door and pushed it open. Aaliyah jumped out of the way.

"Oh, so sorry!" Charlie yelled, covering her mouth.

"No worries," Aaliyah responded as she jumped on her bed. The bed creaked as her weight dipped into the extra-long mattress.

"What's up! I didn't see you last night!" Charlie lunged onto her bed, slightly less graceful than Aaliyah.

Aaliyah had heard Charlie come in around nine o'clock. She pretended to be asleep once she heard the keys in the door and kept her eyes on the eggshell paint until she heard Charlie's light snores. Then she went to the lounge for the rest of the night and completed two weeks' worth of homework.

Keisha always said it's better to be productive than to let your mind dwell on something you can't change, Aaliyah had thought as she fought sleep.

After watching Aaliyah zone out for an awkward amount of time, Charlie continued, "I saw Jeremiah on the way back from lunch. What'd you do after you both were done with interview prep?" She opened a Ziploc bag and popped a Cheez-It into her mouth.

"Honestly, Charlie," Aaliyah sighed until there was no longer breath in her lungs, "I've been working on finding the individuals that vandalized the BCC," she said in one shallow breath.

Charlie's mouth dropped open and Aaliyah could see the cheese remains covering her usually white teeth. "You've *what?*"

Aaliyah shook her head, "But even if I find out who it is, I don't think anybody would believe me." Aaliyah's voice was weak. She broke down in the middle of their twelve-by-nineteen dorm room floor. Exhaustion and defeat led her to release the sob she had been holding in since the previous morning.

Aaliyah felt an arm around her, and Charlie gently pulled Aaliyah into her boney shoulder. "I believe you," she cooed. Charlie remained on the floor supporting Aaliyah's body until her sobs turned into sniffles. Aaliyah lifted her head from the crook of Charlie's neck. She felt lighter as she lifted her body from Charlie's. She wiped her runny nose and wiped her under eyes with her pajama shirt.

Charlie rubbed a thumb over Aaliyah's left knuckle—something Aaliyah's mom did to comfort her too.

Charlie turned her body to face Aaliyah and crossed her legs. "I want to help."

Aaliyah gave her a bewildered side-eye.

Charlie straightened her posture. "I want to help," she said more adamantly.

Aaliyah turned her body too. "Charlie…" Aaliyah began dismissively.

Charlie held her hand up, "Before you deny me, this is when I can use my privilege to our advantage. People will be more trusting of me. There are more White people willing to give me information because they think I'm as ignorant as them. But really, I'm here for you."

Aaliyah took a few moments. Charlie had a point no matter how disappointing the reality of the situation was.

"Okay. I'll go over what the plan was. If you have any ideas for a plan B, feel free to share. But before I do that, I need to include somebody else that has already helped." Aaliyah lifted herself from the carpeted floor that covered six weeks' worth of dust. She took her phone off the charger and called Jeremiah.

He answered after the second ring, "What's up?" His voice was raspy.

Aaliyah's voice went an octave higher. "Hey, you busy?"

Charlie leaned past Aaliyah's shoulders to try and see who Aaliyah was talking to.

Aaliyah waved her off and turned around so she couldn't see her blushing. "Nah, I'm free for the next hour. You good?"

Aaliyah looked at her unruly cuticles. "Yeah, I'm fine." Aaliyah retuned to the floor with Charlie who had not moved from her seated position. Aaliyah put the phone on speaker. "I'm here with Charlie."

Charlie leaned toward the phone. "Hi," she chirped.

Jeremiah chuckled, "Hey Charlie. What are you two ladies up to?"

"I'm including Charlie in on our plan—or, my plan. She wants to help, and I think she can." Aaliyah fell silent while she waited for Jeremiah's answer.

"I agree. Let's go over how the meeting went yesterday and we can go from there."

Aaliyah didn't realize she was holding her breath until she released it.

Aaliyah began the story from when she walked back to the dorm after seeing the BCC. Charlie had a range of shocked facial expressions when Aaliyah recounted her observations of Grayson and then the Dean. Jeremiah was silent on the other end until Aaliyah ended, "So, I don't know where to go from here."

Jeremiah and Charlie remained silent while they processed the details.

"I have a suggestion," Charlie shyly broke the silence. "You could attend the open forum tonight. You could speak your mind *and* present your evidence. You can speak without interruption and have an audience that I'm sure will support you."

Aaliyah nodded. *Not bad*, she thought.

Jeremiah spoke into the phone, "I agree with Charlie. But we have to be more strategic with what you're going to say. Because if you just go off, then they'll have you escorted off stage in a minute! Me and Charlie are gonna see your ass on stage. 'Security, get yo' hands off me!'"

Aaliyah pictured him mimicking her with her arms flailing around. Charlie laughed.

Aaliyah rolled her eyes. "Then what do you suggest I do, genius?"

The phone was silent. "I think you should revise their email."

Aaliyah and Charlie looked at each other simultaneously with a confused look. "I should what?"

"Remember in class, you were saying they included 'Moving Forward' in the email without even acknowledging the root of the issue?"

Aaliyah recalled, "Yeah."

"Well, talk about how they should properly handle racial encounters. Emphasize that there are *racist* intentions and Black students do not feel safe on campus. Especially when administration will only protect students that resemble them."

Aaliyah understood. "So, I should talk about what their email should have said and the actions they need to take now."

"Exactly."

Charlie reinserted herself into the conversation. "But what about the evidence for the case? Do we leave that alone?"

Aaliyah's accomplished feeling was short-lived. She paused to think. "What if we threaten them?"

Aaliyah heard rustling on Jeremiah's end. "We're not doing that."

Charlie gave her a baffled expression.

Aaliyah shook her head. "Not physically. How about I tell them that if they don't meet our demands, then we will create some sort of movement that lets Black students know the discrimination they'll face at a university you pay your money to."

A few seconds went by while all three considered the plan. "Alright. I'm good with that."

Charlie followed his lead. "Yeah, me too. Aaliyah… You understand if you say these things, it could provoke other African American students to revolt too."

Jeremiah added to Charlie's point, "Yeah, you may be the face of a revolution you didn't necessarily mean to cause."

Aaliyah considered their point. She wanted to call Keisha and tell her everything she had done so far but she didn't want her to be involved.

"Yeah. I'm ready."

No more throwing rocks, Dr. Robinson, she thought.

* * *

Aaliyah stepped into the auditorium they had set up for the open forum. There were hundreds of seats set up. Extra string lights were set along the outside aisles. She saw volunteers walking with folded chairs earlier when she went to class. A few of them had on "Black Lives Matter" shirts.

The stage had a microphone placed in the middle that stood like a brave soloist. A few feet away from the microphone were two women of color and a Hispanic male sitting in a row of seats. The White woman sitting in the first chair had her own microphone underneath her chair. She had brown hair layered to her shoulders. She had wrinkles that made her look older than she probably was. She had on a paisley printed shirt that went to her midthigh, paired with black leggings and black Toms. As Aaliyah walked down the aisle, the microphone reflected in her face. She looked back at the stage again. To the right of the White woman was a Black woman Aaliyah had not seen before. She had locs and a daishiki paired with black leggings and black running shoes. Aaliyah had never seen her at any BCC events.

Aaliyah noticed her hands trembling once she heard the paper rattling. She had a fresh piece of notebook paper that had her points written down for her speech.

Jeremiah tapped Aaliyah's shoulder. He pointed down the row she was about to walk by. There were fifteen minutes before the forum began, but people were flooding in by the second. Aaliyah saw four seats in the middle of the row, so she led her friends down. They each plopped down in their seat and Aaliyah took off her jacket to place it in the seat to her right.

Aaliyah turned to tell Charlie and Jeremiah that she was saving that seat for Kiley, but Jeremiah was already facing her.

Jeremiah smirked. "I'm proud of you. You're trying to make a change. I knew I saw something special in you when we were at that booth."

Aaliyah was glad the auditorium was dimly lit because she was sure she was blushing. She pecked him on the cheek as a thank you. She reverted her attention back to her notes, mouthing each point and telling herself the rest would be improvised.

Suddenly, there was a loud, thumping noise echoing in the building. The audience groaned and looked around to find who was making the noise. It was the White woman with wrinkles. She was standing cheerily at the microphone placed at the middle of the stage. She kept the same smile until the audience of seven hundred people quieted down.

"Good evening, students of Bellpoint University. My name is Kristy Beth, and I will be the host this evening. Before we open the forum up for Black students, I would like to begin the evening by introducing a dear friend of mine, Christine Bower."

The audience gave a faint applause as the Black woman approached the microphone. "Good evening students, faculty, and administration. Thank you for coming to this open forum today to discuss the tragic event that was set to attack Black students. Unfortunately, the act was committed, but how we can move on as a university is up to the ones that have joined us today."

Aaliyah noticed a few people in the audience nodding their heads.

Christine continued, "Which is why I would like to start off the conversation with Black students. The goal today is to amplify their voices and ensure we listen to their grievances. With that, I will leave the microphone to any student that would like to speak."

She walked back to her seat with a beaming Kristy giving her two thumbs up.

Aaliyah scanned the crowd. Her eyes landed on a Black girl who looked her age. Aaliyah watched her shoulders lift to her small ears and slowly sink back. She got up from her seat after her deep breath and walked to the side ramp of the stage. Every pair of eyes followed as she walked to the stage. Her eyes remained on the microphone her entire journey.

The girl was average height. She was wearing jeans and a gray shirt that had an image over the right breast pocket. Once she arrived at her destination, she looked at her empty seat. The friend that was sitting near her made a heart with her hands. The girl took another deep breath and began, "We read *To Kill a Mockingbird* and are told that Atticus was the hero, but I always thought it was Tom. We're taught that

Lincoln freed the slaves but were never told he requested they be sent back to Africa after he won the war. We're told the Constitution is the foundation of our country, but slaves built the entire country. We're told we'll get another Black Community Center, and concerns are dismissed and burned down just like that building. Fears I am consumed by. I contemplate…whether I belong here—whether I should have attended an HBCU. But when I applied, they said 'We need you!' Well, now I know what they need. A met quota and my tuition money."

The room's attention was commanded after the young woman's first line of her spoken word. She ended her final word with such emphasis Aaliyah felt a chill. The crowd erupted in applause as she walked off the stage, only making eye contact with the ground. Once she returned to her seat, people were still clapping. Aaliyah noticed her shy persona was overwhelmed with the pats on her back and praises from rows near her. She'd set the tone.

The applause did not fade until Kristy walked up to the microphone the young girl was at. Aaliyah noticed she did not join the applause, her face contorted into a disappointed look.

"Wow, what a beautiful poem. But unfortunately, this open forum is for the purpose of Black students expressing their grievances *and* possible improvements to the university. But thank you so much for starting us off!" Kristy held her hand out to the girl who was still being praised.

Aaliyah heard the footsteps of another person approaching the side entrance of the stage. Jeremiah and Aaliyah's mouth dropped when they saw who was quickly approaching the microphone like she was ready to bulldoze Kristy off the stage: Kiley.

Kristy almost hopped out of the way and returned to her seat when Kiley snatched the corded microphone out of the stand.

"Hi, y'all. My name is Kiley Thomas and, honestly, I wasn't going to speak today, but now I know I need to. Excuse my language, but this is bullshit—"

Kristy swiftly reached underneath her chair and interrupted Kiley, "Please refrain from cursing! That goes for all participants, thank you." She brushed her feathered brown hair from her eyes and scoffed, suddenly looking like she regretted hosting the event.

Kiley side-eyed the host and continued. "That's why I said excuse my language."

Kiley said it softly into the microphone but loud enough that the first few rows could hear her. Aaliyah saw the shakes of shoulders from people chuckling.

"Black students, the *few* Black professors, and Black admin are intentionally attacked, yet we're the ones that are asked for solutions. We're not allowed time to grieve, mourn, or heal from the loss of the only safe space we have on campus. No! We're asked to attend this open forum. What if Black students don't want to have open dialogue right now. We just lost our resource center for heaven's sake! The reiteration of a 'safe space for open dialogue' is a farce because the people that vandalized the property could be in this room right now."

Kiley paused to take a breath from her ramble. While she paused, the audience gave her a few cheers.

Kiley's wrinkled eyebrows relaxed at the signs of encouragement. "Black students should not be allowed to be the victims and the healers. It makes the college experience exponentially more difficult and many of us lack the guides and support our White counterparts have. So, how can we do better as a university? Increase representation not only in the student population but in higher positions of power so we *actually* feel like somebody is fighting for us."

Aaliyah and Jeremiah jumped to their feet. Their echoed claps and energy incited other audience members to join until the entire auditorium was cheering for Kiley. Kiley's fair skin blushed pink as she walked back down the ramp. She saw Jeremiah and Aaliyah jumping, trying to flag her down. She walked down their aisle and was bombarded with whispers of congratulatory statements. Kiley removed Aaliyah's jacket and sat down in her seat beaming. A wave of students began lifting from their seats to approach the stage. A line formed with eager students encouraged to share their stories.

Charlie, Jeremiah, Aaliyah, and Kiley were engaged throughout each story every student shared. After the seventh student spoke, an older Hispanic woman approached from the shadows. She shyly approached the microphone as her heels clicked across stage.

"Hello, everybody," she waved to the audience. Her voice was warm with a Spanish accent.

"I want to thank the organizers for hosting this event. Having this conversation is just as necessary as protecting Black students." Aaliyah recognized the sincerity in her eyes.

"I have been a Spanish professor at the university for eleven years—"

"We love you, Senora Henry!" Three students said in unison. A few cheers followed their interruption.

The woman waved off the students with a laugh. "Thank you," she replied. "But I must say how the university addresses hate crimes against their own students is shameful."

There were a few individual whoops from the audience.

"It saddens me because students will come into my class a day after something terrible has happened, and they're expected to learn? We cannot expect our students to be robots in an educational setting that is supposed to teach and provide them with experience that will prepare them for the world. Every time we fail to acknowledge racism exists on our campus, we fail each and every one of our students. We allow non-Black students to believe it doesn't exist when we don't say the word—racism."

She took a pause and sighed into the microphone. "I had a student a few years ago. He was energetic, charismatic, a great participant—overall a very sweet boy. One day he came into class and was distant. He avoided classmates. His energy was off and I could tell. I told the class I would be meeting with each student about their final project presentations individually. I called him outside first but instead of asking him about the project, I asked if he would allow me to know what was concerning him that day. He agreed and told me his brother had passed away at home." Her voice cracked and she took a step away from the microphone. The entire room was silent.

She began fanning her watery eyes, "I was astounded for a moment because here he is grieving, yet still attending my class. He went on to tell me that after his mom told him his brother died, she proceeded to tell him that she couldn't pay for college and his brother's funeral. It broke my heart. So, he told me he called the academic advisors before my class and they referred him to financial aid and so on and so forth. They told him he might as well drop out." She pinched her sweater with her fingers and brought the cuff of her sleeve to her eyes. She dapped her tears before she continued. "The rest of class, we searched for ten different scholarships, and I wrote him a letter of recommendation for every. Single. One."

The audience applauded the professor. She waited until it ended. "It baffled me that I, a professor that has taught at a university for eleven years, helped a student more than the resources that are *required* to help him did. It made me wonder, who else may not have had a professor that simply checked on them? Now he is a mechanical engineer at the company he had aspired to be at his entire life. I understand today's intention was to amplify Black voices, and I clearly am not Black, but I wanted to ask the university as a professor, woman of color, wife, representative of this university, to go the extra mile for students simply because they deserve to be protected."

Chants of "Senora Henry!" flooded the room. She walked off the stage with an elegance Aaliyah had never seen. Mascara streaks lined her cheeks, but the illumination of the lights glowed upon her cheeks. Her sweater flowed behind her until she disappeared out of Aaliyah's view. Aaliyah heard sniffles from a couple students behind her. Aaliyah checked to see the time—6:57 p.m. She glanced at the line, noticing there were no students. She rose from her chair while Kristy mirrored her. Aaliyah used her long legs to her advantage and reached the end of the line marker before Kristy reached the microphone.

Kristy Beth leaned into the microphone, "We are coming to the closing of our forum today. After this, young lady, you may send any further concerns to our counselors or Dean of Students, Katy Palmer." Kristy flashed a smile at Aaliyah and waved her forward.

Aaliyah side-eyed the host. She felt like she could not trust a person with two first names. A frivolous rule Damien had told her when she was seven. One that had coincidentally never steered her wrong. "Hi." Aaliyah began shakily.

Unexpectedly, she was more nervous after she looked at her friends sitting in the fifth row. There was a sea of rows behind them that disappeared into the dark. Every single chair was filled, and people were sitting knee to knee. She even saw figures standing in the back, the wall supporting their weight. Her mind went blank as the stares began to overwhelm her. Aaliyah scanned the crowd and her eyes landed on Dr. Robinson standing in the bottom left corner. Aaliyah pleaded with her eyes and Dr. Robinson answered with an encouraging nod. Dr. Robinson straightened her posture and protruded her chin. Aaliyah mimicked her actions.

"Hello," she began more confidently. "As a freshman, I too was disappointed in the response the university had to this act dedicated to hate. But to add to the disappointment, my older friends, mentors, and administration were not shocked by the response. The email claimed they're reminded of the words of Dr. Martin Luther King, of words resonating with hope. But in reality, they found words of dismissal. The university attempts to placate Black people and people of color when it comes to issues of hate, but I'm here to say you can't dismiss us anymore!"

The crowd began cheering. Aaliyah noticed a few students leaning away from their chairs, eager to hear more.

"The words I'm reminded of from Dr. Martin Luther King are the ones from his 'I Have a Dream' speech. 'Let us not be satisfied. Let us not be satisfied with one verdict. Let us not be satisfied with just a taste of justice. Let us not be satisfied until justice rolls down like water and righteousness like a stream.' We've seen people of authority fail their students time and time again. We're not only asking you to create a safe environment for students of all demographics but to *listen* to what we ask of you. We're asking to not only offer support when acts of violence are made against us but to have more dialogue for those that need it—meaning White staff, administration, professors. Then and only then will I believe this is a university that truly does not tolerate hate."

Kristy shifted uncomfortably in her seat. She began nervously nodding her head at the crowd's response. A moment passed before she snapped her head back at Aaliyah. She politely crossed her legs and placed her hands over her knees. Aaliyah pulled out a neatly folded notebook paper from her back pocket. She took a deep breath as the silence increased her heartbeat. She began, "As a result of feeling neglected by a university that I pay tuition to, pay for resources to, and expect to earn a degree from, I have created a list of demands." Aaliyah did not dare look at the crowd. She read the first point, "One: I want the university to hire a dean specifically for students of color. Somebody that is specifically looking out for *us*. Two: I would also like the Black Community Center to be rebuilt by the beginning of next semester *and* for Black students be allowed to request extra additions to the center. Three: I ask that every academic class be required to discuss the racist actions students on this campus committed. If need be, a template that guides the conversation can be created and provided."

Aaliyah felt the sadness she'd felt when she witnessed the destruction of the BCC, the hostility she felt toward those boys on the sidewalk, and the defeat after she spoke to the dean. All her emotions led her to take the mic from the stand and directly face the three hosts. All three of their bodies stiffened, and their eyes widened like kids that had been caught by their parents. Aaliyah looked in Kristy's eyes. "We go through so much trauma just to not receive the same treatment as these legacies do." She refocused her attention to all three. "If these demands are not met, I will create a platform where Black students can input their grievances. I will broadcast it, so the entire world will know the complacency of this university. This institution's silence allows students of color to be constantly threatened by uneducated mother—"

Aaliyah's mic cut off. The audience erupted in various shouts of praise and anger toward the hosts. The consensus of Aaliyah's mic being cut off was not approved. As Aaliyah rushed down the stage, she saw a shaggy-haired boy exit the auditorium before she could reach the door. Aaliyah looked behind her to see if Jeremiah, Charlie, or Kiley were behind her but all she saw was students crowding the border of the stage yelling profanities and demands at Kristy. Kristy scrambled to call security and speak into the microphone. "Thank you all for coming! We will go over our next steps soon! *Security*! Please find your way to an exit." Aaliyah stepped out of the auditorium basking in the silence and breeze. She felt accomplished and heard, a feeling that had been unfamiliar lately.

Aaliyah did not have silence for long. A loud alert came to her phone. An unrecognized address had sent her an email. She looked at the notification. Confused yet intrigued, she opened it. The message was sent from an address named: UseThisHowYouWill@Bellpoint.com.

The email had no subject heading, so Aaliyah clicked on the document attached. Her mouth fell open.

"*Yo*! They're going crazy in there. You did the damn thing, Miss X." Jeremiah was the first person to come out of the building, followed by Charlie and Kiley. Their beaming smiles dropped as they made their way around to see Aaliyah's face. She flipped her phone toward her friends and their faces morphed into an expression similar to hers.

NOBODY TELLS YOU: THERE ARE COWARDS

"Aaliyah Harris,

I have been contemplating this decision for some time now. After attending the open forum today, I recognize you're the person I need to share this with. I am providing you with this information below. Do what you will with this information as I will be deleting this account tomorrow. I know the university will not do much about this case unless evidence is presented. I decided to not be one of the 'uneducated motherfuckers' you were talking about today.

Wyatt Palmer

Jacob Johnson

Joseph Lee

Good luck,

Anonymous"

Kiley began walking toward the hallway. "We need to go sit down and figure out what we're going to do with this before the stampede of angry people exit this musty ass building."

The three nodded and Aaliyah led the way toward Coop-era Cafe. The four walked in silence, the gloomy morning reflecting how each felt. Aaliyah spotted a booth in the back and pointed in its direction. Once they were all seated, Aaliyah began. "Okay…"

Kiley shot up from the end of the booth, "Wait hold on!"

They all squinted their eyes at her.

"*What*? I need some energy so we can demolish the mother-effers." Keisha sauntered over to the cafe line.

Charlie bowed her head. "Yeah, me too." She followed Kiley to the short line.

Jeremiah slouched in the seat. "You good?" he asked.

Aaliyah thought about her answer, unable to tell how she felt at the moment. The serotonin she felt after her speech had been crushed with the weight of the email.

She turned to Jeremiah, ready to express the truth of her emotions. Before she was able to answer, a girl interrupted her. "Hi! I was sitting at the other table, and my friend and I wanted to say great speech!" The girl stepped to the side to reveal her friend who remained at the table vigorously waving her hand like a fan.

"Thank you so much," Aaliyah replied warmly.

The girl returned to her table. Aaliyah turned to Jeremiah, "I feel like the intention of my speech has been lost in the demands. I wanted to show pain, anger, and hurt. Now I'm afraid they only heard my demands, and it will create a riot instead of a movement."

Charlie and Kiley both returned to the booth discussing how sweet their strawberry banana smoothies were. After taking another sip, they could feel the melancholy shift at the table.

Kiley saw Aaliyah's drooping face and leaned in. She scooped up Aaliyah's hands, one hand still damp from the smoothie cup. "It may not be how you want. But we're going to initiate some change. We all have each other's back. With our great minds together—*who's* stopping us?"

Aaliyah smiled at her friend. "Okay! Then let's figure out how we're going to use this."

* * *

Aaliyah and Charlie were elated as they left the cafe. The two went over the plan as they walked back to their dorm. They flashed their ID cards in sync as they walked toward the elevator. Three other girls and a guy were waiting for it as well. They were all chatting cheerily before they glanced back at Aaliyah and Charlie.

The elevator jolted to a stop and the doors opened giving a *whoosh* sound that replaced the sudden silence. They all stepped in, and one girl asked Aaliyah, "What floor?" without acknowledging Charlie.

"Six please," Aaliyah answered.

Aaliyah turned to Charlie to start another conversation as she saw the girl also pressed eight. She noticed two of the girls kept solemnly glancing at each other repeatedly before one stepped forward and cut Aaliyah off. "I just want to say I'm sorry on behalf of all of us." She gestured toward everybody in the elevator—including Charlie.

Charlie cocked her head to the side and gave her a bewildered look.

Aaliyah knew what she was referencing and decided to play. "It's okay, I know the athletes live on the eighth floor; just bring some spray deodorant next time."

Charlie's hand flew to her mouth to stifle a laugh. The girl cleared her throat awkwardly. "No. I'm talking about the racial tensions on our campus. I can't believe we're living in times like this still." The girl turned her head toward her friends who nodded in encouragement of her comments.

Another one spoke up, "I thought we were doing better. We even have a Black president!"

Charlie interjected, "Having a Black president does not address the racial plights African Americans have to overcome from the unaddressed truth of Black history. Continuing the excuse of a Black president perpetuates a culture of ignorance because it does not account for our discriminatory institutions."

Aaliyah raised her eyebrow at Charlie and nodded her head in approval once all the attention was no longer on herself. The elevator doors opened to their floor. Charlie's eyes remained on the friend group. "Y'all have a good night though." Aaliyah stepped off the elevator gracefully. Charlie stalked down the hallway close behind.

"I was just trying to apologize—" Aaliyah heard before the doors closed again.

Charlie struggle to get her keys out of her backpack once they reached their door. Aaliyah smiled and nudged Charlie's shoulder twice. Charlie was not smiling in return. She grunted and spun her backpack around her bird-like chest and opened the first two pockets in her backpack. Aaliyah saw the light reflect their silver dorm keys in her water bottle holder.

"Charlie, breathe. They're right here." Aaliyah chuckled and gently grabbed the keys from the opposite pocket. She handed the keys to her roommate.

Charlie responded with a curt "thank you" and placed the keys in the lock. She twisted from the left and then to the right and plunged her shoulder into the door like a linebacker. She bounced back once the door didn't open. Charlie ran her fingers through her hair revealing some layered side bangs Aaliyah hadn't noticed before. She tried again and they both heard the pop from the lock. Charlie repeated the linebacker motion and the door swung open till it dented the wall. Aaliyah quickly shuffled out of the way as the door swung back closed.

Charlie was slightly panting, and Aaliyah wasn't sure if it was from the exertion of energy she used to open their door or their unusual elevator encounter.

"How can people be that *dumb*?" Charlie began emptying her backpack in a frazzled manner. Aaliyah found her answer.

Charlie continued, "To be so blatantly rude and invasive. Honey, you don't need to apologize on my behalf; I'm doing the work so I don't have to be grouped with *that*. And who are they to mention—" Charlie looked up from the ground to see Aaliyah patiently waiting for her to finish ranting.

Charlie's big eyes drooped, "Am I like that?"

Aaliyah quickly dismissed that thought. "No. You handled yourself well. 'Having a Black president does not address the racial plights'" Aaliyah mimicked in a higher pitched voice with her finger waving around. Aaliyah burst out laughing.

"This isn't funny!" Charlie whined. "How did that not make you freaking livid!" Aaliyah could tell Charlie was getting anxious again.

"Charlie," Aaliyah began softly. "That elevator encounter was something I get twice a week. I understand it's unusual for you but that's what I—and a lot of other Black people— deal with daily. People apologizing for this racist world but not doing much to counter those actions. I'm sorry it made you uncomfortable or mad. But I've become numb to ignorance, unfortunately."

Charlie nodded her head in despair. "So you don't want to just jump at their throats every time they say something so insensitive?"

Aaliyah shrugged. "Oh no, I want to," Aaliyah reassured, "but I can't. I'll be the 'angry Black woman,' and the situation will escalate to the point that I'd be in danger. They're never worth that."

Keisha made sure I knew that before I came to campus, Aaliyah thought.

Charlie's forehead scrunched, and it gave Aaliyah a preview of what she may look like in thirty years. "Wow."

Charlie began organizing what she'd dumped out of her backpack. "Oh, by the way, Grayson is coming over to help me with stats; he took it last semester and still has the notes. Is that cool?"

"Well, if he has the notes, can't he just give them to you?" Aaliyah smirked.

Charlie turned pink, "Well yeah, I guess so—"

Aaliyah cut her off, "I'm kidding. Of course, it's fine. I'll be doing homework at my desk."

Aaliyah placed her notebook and laptop on her desk. She carefully placed her earphones in her head and turned on the noise cancelling feature. She flipped her notebook to the plan and began typing it into a locked folder on her computer. She knew she wasn't going to be doing any homework.

After a few minutes into color coordinating each person's job, she heard a knock on the door. Charlie's seat sprang up as she lunged for the door handle. Aaliyah turned to wave at Grayson, but almost jumped when she saw him. He looked like he hadn't rested for days. His under eyes looked a shade away from gray against his pale skin. His hair was disheveled, which Aaliyah had never seen since she noticed hair gel and a comb in his backpack every day at class. His usual style must have been left in his closet as he was wearing sweatpants, a hoodie, and low-top Vans. Aaliyah squinted her eyes at the drawings alongside his shoes. She noticed poorly drawn stars, fire, and something else she couldn't decipher.

Aaliyah thought about asking if he was feeling ill, but decided she had other priorities to attend to. Aaliyah didn't have to look at Charlie to know her disappointed expression. She had applied cherry bomb lip gloss a few minutes before his arrival and asked if her messy bun was "messy-cute or messy-messy." Aaliyah chose a random answer.

Aaliyah turned her headphones up once she heard the term "standard deviation." She typed furiously at the keys as if she was turning in a midterm in ten minutes. After looking over her work several times, she was satisfied.

She swiveled her chair around to ask Charlie to use her printer and almost hit Charlie's knees as Charlie was leaning over to tap her shoulder. Aaliyah pulled out a headphone.

"Sorry, I didn't mean to make you jump. I was just going to tell you that I was going to use the bathroom. I think that smoothie had milk in it. You know how dairy gets me!" Charlie practically limped to the door. Aaliyah laughed, admiring how she was not afraid to comment on her bowel movements in front of her crush. Grayson was laughing too.

Between her laughs, Aaliyah asked, "Can I use your printer?" as Charlie walked out.

The door shut. "Sure!" Charlie shouted back, already halfway down the hallway.

Aaliyah rolled her chair the five feet across the room. She shifted her computer in her lap and connected it to Charlie's printer. It began to hum, and Aaliyah decided to make small talk with Grayson. "So, what grade did you get in Stats last year?"

Grayson smiled to himself, "B minus. And I barely got that. I don't know why she asked for my help."

Aaliyah watched four copies shoot out of the printer. "You know why," she answered.

His cheeks turned the same shade as Charlie's had earlier. "Yeah," he answered shyly.

Aaliyah stood up to grab the papers, towering over him while he sat in the small stool Charlie offered him earlier.

"Is that for Dr. Robinson's end of the semester project? I forgot that's due soon." Grayson asked as he glanced at the papers.

Aaliyah checked the calendar above Charlie's desk. It was due in four weeks; she groaned in response. "No, I haven't started that."

Aaliyah scooted back to her side, thinking the conversation was done.

"Well, everybody's talking about you after the open forum today. I'm sure everybody's expecting something great," Grayson said nonchalantly. He circled another term he wanted to review with Charlie.

Aaliyah lifted her feet from the ground and spun around once again, "Wait. Were you there?"

Grayson's cheeks flushed and slowly turned into a crimson red. Aaliyah had not even seen Charlie reach that shade when she was embarrassed.

He kept his head down toward his stats paper, shielding his face from Aaliyah. "Yeah, I stepped in for a moment but there weren't any seats left so I stood in the back and left shortly after you were done. I had to go to a meeting."

Aaliyah nodded. "Oh, what organizations are you involved in?"

"It was for my frat," He responded quickly.

A beat passed. "OkaW... what frat are you in again?"

"Damn, is this an interrogation?" Grayson chuckled nervously.

Aaliyah grabbed her notes from earlier. She read, "four males, designs on shoes." Aaliyah scooted her chair a couple inches away from Grayson's chair. "It can be."

Grayson faced her, and his shoulders dropped. "Aaliyah."

"You were involved?" She moved her head back.

"My frat brothers made me drive, but I never did any damage," he attempted to explain.

"Yes, you did." Aaliyah's voice bellowed in their small room.

Grayson's eyes dropped to the floor. "I'm sorry, I really am."

Aaliyah grabbed a paper from her folder and slapped it on the table. "You can't be sorry if you helped. You never even came forward!"

Grayson's eyes darted from side to side.

"...You're Anonymous."

His silence gave her an answer.

"You're a coward."

"I'll come to the Dean with you if you don't turn me in." He kept his eyes on the floor. "Please." His head dropped to the level of his shoulders.

"Why should I care what happens to you? I already have all the information I need right here." She waved the paper in the air.

"I didn't give you the other name involved." Grayson looked up like a puppy dog caught doing something wrong.

A set of keys jiggled in the door. Grayson stiffened in response. Aaliyah moved to her desk, still staring at Grayson in disgust.

They were both silent as they waited for Charlie.

"Please don't tell her." Grayson pleaded before she walked in the room.

"Sorry! I was singing while I was in the bathroom and Amanda, this other girl on our floor, came in and said she loved that song too and ..." Charlie caught her breath and saw the tense expressions on her friends' faces.

"We all good?" Charlie asked concerned.

"Yeah. I was telling Grayson how pathetic some people are." Aaliyah answered quickly. She gathered the papers on Charlie's desk, briskly shoving Grayson's items to the side.

"Oh? Like who?" Charlie asked.

Aaliyah released a heavy sigh. "Hopefully nobody that we know." Aaliyah went back to her desk and put in her headphones. She hoped that was indication enough she didn't want to answer Charlie's questions.

Aaliyah balled up the four copies of the plan to the size of her scrunched left fist. She got up from her chair and placed them in the trash can. A jolt of anger shot threw her, but she felt tears welling up. She turned around to face her mirror so Charlie wouldn't see her sudden change of emotions.

Aaliyah stared at herself in the mirror. Her sunken eyes looked as though she hadn't slept for days. Her usual swagger had disappeared as the effort to look presentable faded into the effort to wake up. Her forehead was oily which made her dry, cracked lips stand out. Her skin looked a couple shades lighter from the lack of sunlight. She looked as exhausted as she felt.

Aaliyah felt a pair of eyes on her that weren't her own. She locked eyes with Grayson through his black computer screen. He looked almost as sad as Aaliyah did gazing in the mirror. Aaliyah wasn't sure if it was pity? Regret? Fear?

Aaliyah's sadness was quickly replaced with hatred. She went back to her chair and flipped open her laptop. She went to her email and clicked "Reply."

"Dear 'Anonymous,'

Meet me at the quad tomorrow at 9 a.m. or you will be exposed.

Sincerely,

Aaliyah Harris"

Before Aaliyah pressed send, she reached underneath her desk and pulled out the miniature mirror Keisha had gifted her before she left. She slammed the mirror on her desk and angled it so she could see Grayson clearly. She sent her message and paused her "Punch the Wall" playlist. She saw Grayson's phone light up and, as Charlie tossed her head back from another joke of his, he pushed it deeper in his pocket.

NOBODY TELLS YOU: PROTEST PREPARATION

Aaliyah tapped her foot impatiently as she waited. She checked her phone: 8:04 a.m. She glanced around the empty hallways and remembered to send a text to Jeremiah.

> I'm at the student union waiting for him. I'll text you how it went.

Aaliyah tried to relax in her chair. The empty campus was quiet. All she heard was the whistle of the breeze on that calm Sunday. She was sure students were still recovering from their Saturday nights this morning. A shadowed figure approached from behind her seat and Grayson sat down in the chair across from her. He looked like he was recovering himself.

"You're late," she grumbled.

"I had to make sure you had all of these." He aggressively unzipped his backpack and tossed a stack of papers on the desk. Grayson moved slightly and hit Aaliyah's knee. The small table did not accommodate their long legs.

Aaliyah snatched the papers and began analyzing them; they were printed screenshots of a text thread between two phone numbers. Aaliyah returned her gaze to Grayson.

He shrugged. "I had to go through a lot of shit for that."

"Good," Aaliyah mumbled in response. She pointed at the sent text messages.

"Wyatt Palmer, president of the fraternity."

Aaliyah nodded trying to connect more clues.

"Also the Dean of Students's son."

Aaliyah paused. "*Dean Palmer*?"

Grayson looked disappointed he couldn't reveal that information to Aaliyah himself. He adjusted his seated position in the cold metal chairs. "Yeah. How'd you know that?"

"Because I tried to meet with that heffa' before." Aaliyah tried to refrain from making too many comments before she frightened Grayson from giving her the information she needed. Aaliyah pointed to the receiving number.

"Jacob Johnson, another member of the fraternity, Wyatt's best friend. Once you get to page four, those are text messages between Wyatt and his mother."

Aaliyah gave Grayson a disgusted look. He pursed his lips and raised his eyebrows.

She started to flip through the papers reading and rereading every text message.

Grayson stopped her reading. "Did you tell her?"

Aaliyah looked up from the handful of papers, knowing he meant Charlie. She tilted her head to the side and sighed. She realized her feelings of anger had not subsided once Grayson was back in her presence. "Before I answer that, I want to ask you this. If you care so much about what other people think of your poor actions, why did you do it?"

Grayson began to tear at a lonesome piece of paper from the fringed edges of his notebook. "I'm gonna tell you what happened that night because you deserve an explanation."

Aaliyah wasn't sure if she was ready to hear a confession, but she found herself nodding.

"It was Friday, the last night of Hell Week. Wyatt, Jacob, Joseph, and Brandon were all discussing something in a corner. A week before Hell Week began, it felt like we were already enduring the pain once Jacob lost his presidency campaign to Christian—"

Aaliyah interrupted, "I've heard about him. He's been a BCC leader since he was a sophomore."

"And now he's the student body president." Grayson cut his eyes to the side.

"Jacob came back from the election night drunk and complaining about how the last few student body presidents were...African American." He looked at Aaliyah in a way that let her know those were not the words used. Grayson continued, "That night all of the boys ordered us to get beers. They got even more drunk and were rambling about how they had to 'do something about it.'" Grayson scoffed at the comment.

"Idiots," he said under his breath. "Jacob ordered the pledges to sit in these steel chairs that they numbered at the beginning of the week. Once we sat, they blindfolded us. Next thing we know, we're getting swatted in the stomach with what I later learned was the end of a broom...one I'm sure they've never used. After I heard the yelps of the other boys stop, I heard whispers again. They ordered number four to stand up—that was me. I stood up and somebody pried open my hand. Before I knew it, I was being shoved down the hallway leading to 'The Garage.'"

Grayson paused to emphasize "The Garage." Aaliyah gave him a bewildered look. "You don't know what 'The Garage' is?" He returned her confused expression.

Aaliyah gave an annoyed sigh, "No."

"'The Garage' is where all the top frat members keep their cars. You won't see anything in there that's below the price of a 2019 BMW." Grayson opened his water bottle to take a sip.

"Oh."

Grayson made a quenched noise as he sealed his water bottle. "Exactly."

Grayson's shoulders dropped. "I heard a few shuffles and car doors opening and closing. After that, they tore the blindfolds off. They tossed me the keys to a Land Rover Range Rover, and I got in the driver's seat. The rest of the pledges were ordered to stay there. I got in the driver's seat, and I heard the trunk slam and soon after that Wyatt, Jacob, and Joseph were in the car. Everybody was talking over each other, so I sat there quietly. I started getting nervous because I knew it wasn't anything good."

That doesn't make me feel bad for you, Aaliyah thought.

Grayson cut into Aaliyah's thoughts, "Then Wyatt yelled at me, 'Drive bitch! Take us to the BCC!' I didn't exactly know how to get there so Jacob called Kennedy Smith. He was sober enough to give me directions. I drove pretty quickly so I could get whatever they were about to do over with."

Grayson made eye contact with Aaliyah for the first time since beginning his story. He reached his hands out. Aaliayh snatched her hands back and put them into her lap. He looked at the ground disappointedly. "Aaliyah, if I would have known what the intention was, I wouldn't have taken them there."

Aaliyah saw the sincerity in his eyes but pulled her hands away. She needed to hear the rest of the story. "Just keep going."

Grayson sniffed the cold air. "I couldn't even put the car in park before they all hopped out. They grabbed baseball bats, spray paint, and Lucas had a bag of explosives that he got from a friend. Everything happened so fast." He shook his head, turning paler than the gray sky.

Aaliyah chose not to interrupt. She felt a twist in her stomach that she recognized as sickly anger. Before coming to meet with Grayson, she had secretly hoped he felt sickly guilty.

Grayson took a quick breath. "I just sat in the car and watched in shock. I was silent for the first five minutes, questioning what they were doing there or what frat I was really pledging for. Shit, I'm sure the thought of getting caught crossed my mind too. The shock paralyzed me while guilt consumed me."

Grayson scratched his head, stuck in the past moment. He looked back at the ground, "They came back, and their musty bodies brought me out of my paralyzed state." His smile quickly dropped after not seeing Aaliyah crack a smile.

"I contemplated leaving before that of course, but I knew they would blame the entire situation on me if I left them. It was around four in the morning, so the campus was completely dead. They all dashed in the car, slammed the door shut and looked out the windows like little kids seeing Santa Claus in the sky. I couldn't figure out what they were staring at until a few seconds went by and the explosives went off. Within ten seconds, the entire building was destroyed. Every window, shattered. Television sets, projects, monitors, cameras—destroyed. I saw Joseph, who's the artist of the group, spray paint some heinous derogatory terms at the entrance and on the back wall of the building." Grayson couldn't make eye contact with Aaliyah. He was red with embarrassment.

"What did it say?"

"Aaliyah, I don't think—"

"What did it say?" Aaliyah's jaw clenched. She tried to keep her fury contained as Grayson's story continued but she was reaching her limit.

"The entrance said 'WE DONT WANT YOU HERE' and the back walls said…" He gestured his hand forward.

"So those were the words they spray painted off of the sidewalk," Aaliyah said with her jaw still clenched.

Grayson glanced at Aaliyah and nodded his head. "They got back in the car, and they were breathing hard from all the damage they had just done."

Literally and figuratively, Aaliyah thought.

Grayson looked up at the clear sky. "I was instructed to drive back to the house. On the way back, they were saying things like, 'They don't deserve that shit anyway' and 'They only got here because of affirmative action.' Then Wyatt said through his slurred words, 'They get everything they want. Elected campaigns, scholarships, awards just so the university can promote diversity. It's bullshit. I deserve those things too.' They all shouted 'yeah!' like imbeciles, one idiot after the other. As I pulled back into 'The Garage,' Jacob wrapped his arm around my neck and the headrest and whispered in my ear 'Don't tell anybody about this shit or we'll ruin your fucking life.'"

Grayson instinctively placed his shoulder by his ear. Aaliyah looked at Grayson in horror.

"I can still feel the trail of sweat he left by my ear." Grayson gave a half-hearted chuckle.

Grayson opened his mouth, but Aaliyah wanted to know more information. "How many pledges were there?" she asked sternly.

Grayson glanced at her clenched fists placed on the table. "There were five of us before one dropped after he heard about what happened."

Aaliyah slammed her fist on the table, "*Why* aren't you saying their names?" Aaliyah sounded desperate when she intended to sound firm. Her voice cracked at the end of her question. She took a deep breath and counted to three like Keisha told her to do when she was overwhelmed.

Grayson sat still until Aaliyah's eye contact returned to his. Aaliyah rubbed her left knuckle with her right thumb. She tried again, "You said you were going to tell me everything." Aaliyah did not plan to be on the verge of tears, but she felt the tears rising.

"Aaliyah, they didn't choose to be involved. I'm trying to get the ones who *did* this, not—"

Aaliyah scooted back her chair. The steel on the concrete left an echoing screeching sound and a long gray mark on the floor. She had heard enough.

* * *

Jeremiah opened his door. His swollen eyes let Aaliyah know she had just woken him up. "Aaliyah, I don't know what you meant to say in that last text."

Aaliyah pulled up the chair at his apartment's dinner table. She sat down and placed her elbows on the table. She ignored the discomfort of being in the unfamiliar environment. She needed comfort.

"'He's such a coward, I can't STANDSHIN?'" Jeremiah asked while rubbing his eye.

"He's such a coward, I can't stand him," Aaliyah responded curtly.

He went over to sit across from her at the table. "Tell me how it went."

Jeremiah sat and listened to Aaliyah's recap for fifteen minutes. He occasionally nodded his head and allowed Aaliyah to describe Grayson's mannerisms without interruption.

"And then I came here," Aaliyah finished, almost out of breath.

"Okay, what did he tell you to do with that information?"

"He didn't tell me what to do! He just told me what information he wanted me to know." Aaliyah's chest rose and fell quickly. She was on the verge of a panic attack.

Jeremiah noticed the tension in her hands. "Okay, I think we should go to the campus police. I'll go with you, and we can do it together."

Aaliyah appreciated the company Jeremiah offered her. She relaxed her jaw that she realized was still clenched. "Let me get the papers."

Jeremiah smiled at her. "Alright, let me change and we can go." He got up from his chair and walked in the direction of his room.

Aaliyah smiled to herself. "And some deodorant!" she yelled as he walked into his room.

He poked his head out and placed his hand on his heart with a frown. They both laughed in unison.

Aaliyah searched for some gum in her backpack once she heard Jeremiah's electric toothbrush turn on. She saw her phone light up from a notification. She pulled it out to see nine missed calls from Charlie and three text messages. Aaliyah immediately clicked on the messages.

Did you see the campus news?

Did you know about this?

Where are you?

"Jeremiah! Can I turn on your TV?" Aaliyah said while scrambling to find the remote.

"Yeah, it's on my nightstand," Jeremiah responded through his closed bathroom door.

Aaliyah dashed in his room and snatched up the remote.

"Damn! Hold on, Flash! America's Next Top Model comes on at eight. You got time." Jeremiah laughed to himself.

Aaliyah ignored him and turned to channel four.

The same news reporter that reported the destruction of the BCC flashed on the screen. "Today, seven boys were arrested for the destruction of the Black Community Center here at Bellpoint University." The television transitioned to all the boys walking out of their fraternity house in handcuffs with their heads hung low. Aaliyah saw Dean Palmer sobbing and being held back by a couple police officers. Aaliyah's mouth dropped open. Jeremiah swung the door open with his toothbrush hanging out of his mouth.

"An anonymous student reported to have witnessed the incident and turned in the young men this morning. The university is waiting to announce the extent of this prosecution and what will happen to these students. Tune back in tomorrow morning, my name is Karen—"

Jeremiah shut off the TV. Aaliyah didn't notice he had taken the remote from her hands. He shuffled back into the bathroom and then sat on his bed. He leaned back on his elbows with the same shocked look on his own face.

Aaliyah sat on his bed. She remained in her seated position as she started to feel lightheaded.

"I guess we don't have to go to campus police anymore."

Aaliyah cracked a smile. "Jeremiah, do you think h …" she peered into his eyes searching for reassurance.

Jeremiah laid back and stared at the ceiling. "I don't know. But I do know there's no reason for you to put your life or education on the line anymore."

Aaliyah sighed in response. She knew he was right, but she wanted to know. They both sat there in silence for a few minutes. The mixture of shock and relief was setting in.

Jeremiah jumped up from his bed and pointed to his shower. "I'll be out in a few."

Aaliyah gave him a thumbs up as he closed the door. She heard the shower turn on and then heard another buzz from her phone. She jumped up to grab it as she remembered the notifications from Charlie. She clicked on her contact and called. Charlie picked up after the first ring. Aaliyah put her on speaker.

"*Did you see it?*" Charlie bellowed in the phone.

Aaliyah yanked her ear away from the phone. "Yeah," Aaliyah replied with the opposite demeanor of Charlie's.

"*Who* do you think turned them in? Do you think they're gonna go to jail? One of them was the Dean of Students's son! Can you *believe* this?" Charlie sounded elated. Aaliyah knew when she rambled, she was excited. Aaliyah heard the news clip replaying in the background.

"Wyatt Palmer, yeah." Aaliyah placed the phone between her ear and shoulder. She tried to decipher whether Jeremiah's bed was comfortable or if the exhaustion had caught up with her. She lay flat on the bed and closed her eyes as Charlie described how she found out about the news.

"And then that's when I saw them being escorted out by handcuffs, which is when I called you."

Aaliyah replied "Mm-hmm" like a bored husband.

"Why…don't you sound relieved?" Charlie's voice dropped to a slight whisper.

"I don't know. I'm exhausted." Aaliyah put her elbow over her eyes to shield the light peeking through the cracked shades.

"Well—" Charlie attempted to cut in.

"Justice is a farce, Charlie. How can I feel elated when we still don't have a center? I still don't feel safe."

"I get that, but don't you think—"

"And this campus doesn't seem to do much until a White boy confesses."

Aaliyah's eyes shot open as she felt a tap on her knee. Jeremiah's curls were dripping onto his worried face. "She doesn't know that," he mouthed.

Aaliyah slapped her hand over her mouth. She only heard silence.

"Aaliyah, who are you talking about." Charlie's typical cheery voice had disappeared.

"Um…" Aaliyah tried to think of a quick lie.

"Who are you talking about?" Charlie repeated adamantly.

Jeremiah's eyes widened as Aaliyah continued to sit there in silence.

"Charlie, I spoke to Grayson this morning and he told me about the vandalism that night," Aaliyah said through a long sigh.

"How does Grayson know that?" Charlie's voice sounded small.

"He was there, Charlie." Aaliyah admitted.

"*What*? Then why isn't he being arrested too?"

"He said it was forced…and he, um, didn't really want to be there," Aaliyah struggled through her explanation.

"Why didn't you tell me?" Charlie sounded disappointed.

"It was just this morning. And he asked me not to—" Aaliyah pleaded.

"I don't care what he asked! The boy I liked is a criminal and you didn't tell me! Do you not think I can handle that?" Charlie's voice rose but she sounded hurt.

"Charlie, I needed to do this myself!" Aaliyah shot back.

"*Who* said that? You claim you need to do this by yourself, but you are surrounded by people offering to help you! You can't shut me out when I've never proven you wrong!"

"Well, when I allow you to make your own decision, you picked Grayson—" Aaliyah heard the dial tone. Jeremiah stood to the side of the bed shaking his damp hair into a beat-up towel.

Aaliyah's hands were shaking. "How dare she question my decision right now! I'm not worried about her little boyfriend right now! She's so freaking selfish!" Aaliyah vented to Jeremiah.

Jeremiah removed the towel from around his head. He grabbed his hair sponge on the way to the seven-foot mirror placed behind his door. He began moving the sponge in a circular motion. "Well…why didn't you tell her?"

Aaliyah scrunched her eyebrows. She did not expect him not to acknowledge her statements. She looked at his backside, but Jeremiah paused his brushing and met her eyes in the mirror. "Really think about it."

Aaliyah pulled her knees to her chest and began to reflect about her decisions since Grayson's confession in her room.

"I think since I've gotten here, White people have disappointed me, which makes me keep myself from putting all of my trust in her..." Aaliyah pulled her knees to her chin and thought about Charlie.

Jeremiah finished his hair and smiled at himself in the mirror. His phone began to buzz. He smoothly pulled his phone out of his pocket and grinned. "It's Kiley."

He put the phone to his ear, "What's *good!*"

His grin dropped immediately. "Nah, I didn't see it... Oh, for real... Okay..."

Aaliyah stopped reflecting and turned her attention to the phone call. She released her knees and transitioned to a butterfly position.

He better let me take a nap here. Can't go back to the dorm yet, Aaliyah thought while she yawned.

"Nah, I'm with her right now." Jeremiah turned to face Aaliyah. They both watched each other as Jeremiah remained on the phone.

"Is it worse than last year's? Oh wow. Okay. We'll be there. Be safe, see you later." Jeremiah slipped his phone back in his pocket.

He sighed and rubbed his hand over his freshly moisturized face. "They released a statement."

Aaliyah tried to look at him, but Jeremiah averted his eyes. He quietly said, "The boys are on academic probation."

"*What?*" Aaliyah screeched. Jeremiah's roommate banged on their connected wall.

Jeremiah shook his head, "The one boy's dads is one of the top donors for the school. They aren't gonna let that go. He offered to pay for the entire rebuilding of the center."

Aaliyah's lifted her hand to her mouth, and she saw it was shaking. "But they're criminals," she said in a shaky whisper.

Jeremiah shrugged. "Everybody's pissed. Kiley told me campus police have barricaded the doors before the boys come out of the station. Students have gathered around with posters and shit. She thinks it's going to get bad."

Aaliyah felt a jolt of energy. She scooted off the edge of the bed. "We're going."

Jeremiah grabbed her arm before she went out of his room. "Hold on! We need to be safe. Share your location with me."

Aaliyah impatiently pulled out her phone and did as she was asked. Jeremiah eyed Aaliyah's entire outfit. Her five-year-old sweatpants would not shield her from the chilly morning. She had on a graphic T-shirt labeled *Boyz n the Hood*. Her hair was slicked back with a braid. The small amount of concealer she put on that morning did not do much for her tired eyes. She had on high top white leather Converses with gold trim.

Jeremiah snatched the jacket that was on the back of his desk chair. "Here, you may need this."

Aaliyah swung the jacket on her shoulders. "Okay. Thank you. Let's go."

Jeremiah held up both of his hands. "Alright. Let me grab a few things. Wait by the door."

Jeremiah went to his closet and snatched a dry-fit T-shirt from the hanger. He slipped off his slides and put on his tennis shoes. He double knotted them—something he didn't usually do—then slung his backpack over his shoulder. He walked quickly to the kitchen and grabbed a half a gallon of milk and three water bottles. He moved swiftly to the cabinets and ducked under the frame. He threw in aloe vera in the side pocket of his backpack.

Aaliyah waited by the door patiently. She tapped her foot to release her newfound adrenaline. He walked over to her with the backpack swooshing against his T-shirt.

"Hold on," Aaliyah pinched his elbow to stop him.

Jeremiah froze midstep. Aaliyah unzipped his backpack and placed the papers Grayson gave her in his laptop sleeve. She zipped his backpack and gave him the thumbs up. Jeremiah swung the door open on cue. Aaliyah suddenly understood why cats hissed. She squinted her eyes at the sun that had decided to come out. Jeremiah blocked the glare with his hand.

A couple of students ran past them in the hallway. One dropped a couple of items from his full hands and quickly picked them up while his friend ran off in the distance.

"Ayo, bruh!" Jeremiah shouted at him.

The young Japanese boy looked up at Aaliyah and Jeremiah through his thick glasses. He pushed them up the slope of his nose. "Uh, yeah?"

Jeremiah shuffled toward him. "Where y'all going in such a rush?"

The boy's face relaxed. "Oh! The people that destroyed the Black Community Center are being released from the police station. Everybody's going there to boo the police, their parents, them..."

Aaliyah glanced at what was in his hands: a megaphone and goggles.

"Come on, Bradley!" his friend had come back once he noticed they were no longer together.

Bradley shifted the things in his hands, "Be safe!" They both ran off together like escaped convicts.

NOBODY TELLS YOU: WHEN WILL DEMANDS BE MET

———

Aaliyah analyzed her outfit, noting that she didn't have the essential supplies for a protest. Jeremiah invaded her thoughts, "I have supplies in here." He patted his backpack. "And I know where the nearest first aid kit is by the police station."

Aaliyah grinned at him, forgetting the purpose of his preparedness.

Jeremiah led the way. He looked back constantly to check if Aaliyah was keeping up with his pace. Aaliyah focused her attention on the noises that got louder with each step. Students ran past them with signs, steel water bottles, and backpacks. Jeremiah slowed down as the foot traffic increased near the campus police station. Jeremiah pulled his phone out of his pocket and looked back to Aaliyah. He raised his voice over the commotion, "Kiley's near the front. Hold on to my hand. We're gonna weave through this crowd."

Aaliyah nodded and placed her hand in his. The slim fingers that came from her mother slipped delicately into Jeremiah's. He tugged her through the crowd, switching between "Excuse me" and "Sorry" until he found Kiley.

Kiley was in all black. Her black T-shirt was painted in red letters "No Justice, No Peace." Kiley relaxed her disgusted stare at the policemen lined up in front of the police station and gave the two a quick hug.

Jeremiah pointed to her shirt, "I like that."

Aaliyah chimed in, "Yeah, me too."

Kiley pulled the bottom hem of her shirt to gaze at it. "Thanks. My brother and I made it after Trayvon Martin was murdered. The dripping red paint is to symbolize the blood shed from all of the Black lives lost." She ran her finger along the dried paint.

Kiley broke her out of her trance. "Lives that y'all took away!" Kiley shouted in the officer's face. He gazed into the distance. Kiley rolled her eyes and turned back to her friends. "They were in interrogation for two hours."

Jeremiah shook his head. Aaliyah stared at Kiley in astonishment.

Kiley scooted closer to the officers and spoke loud enough for them to hear. "The Central Park Five were interrogated for seven hours for a crime they did not commit. Those spoiled-ass boys are in there for a *couple hours* for a crime they *committed*?"

A few protestors by Kiley chanted, "Yeah!" at her remarks.

Aaliyah heard someone mumble on the officer's walkie talkie. Within a second, the police officer began shoving Aaliyah, Jeremiah, and Kiley to their left. Aaliyah was surrounded by angry shouts of confusion and fear. She stepped out of the way and, across the pathway, saw Bradley and his friend being shoved to their right. A girl in front of Aaliyah fell on her back as the police used excessive force to part the crowd. Aaliyah bent her knees and braced for the impact like Damien taught her.

"Get your hands off me!"

"Aye, bruh!"

"Don't fucking touch me!"

The officers remained silent while the chaos was unfolding. They shoved people with batons, body shields and hands. The doors to the police station cracked open like a whip. Four officers walked out first with the seven boys on their heels. Three officers were behind them, shielding them from the objects that were being thrown from the angry crowd.

The crowd instinctively began shouting at the seven boys involved. Aaliyah saw students on both sides of the split crowd attempting to get through the policemen line. Some debris flew over the heads of people and landed near the boys that were being escorted.

"No justice, no peace!" Kiley chanted. Others followed her lead.

Kiley walked to the top of the steps and pumped her fist to the chant. Soon, everybody was chanting.

Aaliyah noticed heads turning. She was grateful for her height as she peered over the crowd. Bradley was standing on top of the steps, parallel to Kiley. He unclipped his megaphone from his belt loop. "Lock them up! Lock them up!"

A melody of the two chants floated in the air. Aaliyah tried to see if she saw any of the boys' faces as they shuffled together like a shameful flock of sheep. The boys were shoved into a black-tinted Ford Escape.

Officers yelled at a couple students to "Get back!" while they kicked the car's bumper. The officers holding the angry crowd apart released their formation once the boys were safely in the car. Students rushed to the car that had not departed and were banging on the window like anxious fans. Aaliyah got knocked to the side as another protestor ran clumsily to the car.

Aaliyah looked back to see Kiley and Jeremiah watching the commotion. Aaliyah heard tires squeal over the angry shouts. Kiley came down the steps and bumped Aaliyah with her hip. "And just like that."

Aaliyah watched the crowd slowly begin to dissipate. She saw their disappointed faces and posters being thrown away.

Aaliyah forgot Kiley was there when she asked, "Where's Charlie?"

Aaliyah looked down at her shoes and saw two Black footprints on them. "I don't think she'll be here."

Kiley poked her lips out, "Oh."

The police officers began walking back into the station as defeated students began to leave the premises. Aaliyah watched as students of all ethnicities, races, and genders left with their heads hung. She heard conversations of those walking by:

"…And they didn't even get expelled!"

"How am I supposed to feel safe if they let them get away with that."

"I heard one was the Dean's son."

Aaliyah stiffened. She had an idea.

"Jeremiah, do you still see the boy we saw earlier?" Aaliyah took two stairs at a time to peer above the slowly disappearing crowd.

Jeremiah elongated his neck. "Um… Yeah, he's over there by the oak tree talking to somebody."

Aaliyah turned to the direction Jeremiah was pointing. There was a glare from Bradley's megaphone. Aaliyah leaped off the stairs and bounded toward him.

"Hi! May I use your megaphone?" Aaliyah asked quickly. She glanced at the girl he was talking to who looked irritated by Aaliyah's interruption.

"Uh, sure." Bradley unclipped his belt loop.

Bradley and his friend watched as Aaliyah dashed away with the equipment. She leaped up the stairs once more. Aaliyah fidgeted with the buttons on the side of the device. She saw the switch that read "SIREN" and flipped it.

Everybody that was near winced at the sound and plugged their ears.

She flipped the switch back. Everybody was watching her now. Her stomach dropped.

Aaliyah placed her lips a few centimeters away from the screen on the megaphone. "I didn't want to come here."

People shuffled over to the end of the steps to hear Aaliyah clearly. A few students that were leaving returned.

Aaliyah adjusted her grip around the megaphone. "I wanted to go to an HBCU with my friends...but this university offered me financial aid and *promised me* that I would be a valued individual on this campus."

Aaliyah watched as students walking by stopped to hear her. Her nerves resurfaced once she saw more people approaching than the protest. "And today as I stand here today with you all, heartbroken and disappointed, I don't feel valued. I feel like a number."

The growing crowd started an applause. Aaliyah paused, "Today, it's academic probation for vandalism but what about *tomorrow*? Administrators allow a hierarchy of whose voice matters, and I'm here to say no!"

The crowd erupted in cheers and applause.

Aaliyah allowed their energy to resonate within her. "Some of our greatest leaders demanded change. And that's what we need to do today!"

The crowd responded, "Yeah!"

Aaliyah couldn't see the end of the audience. "One of the boys that vandalized the BCC is one of the Dean's children!"

There was an audible gasp from the crowd. Murmurings initiated soon after.

Aaliyah's clenched her toes in her shoes that suddenly seemed too small. She flashed her eyes at Jeremiah. He gave her a supportive smile and mimicked a deep breath.

She repeated his actions and spoke, "I say we start a sit-in at the student union to demand what we deserve!"

An eruption of cheers commenced. Aaliyah nodded her head at the crowd. "We demand more funding for our center! We demand the Dean be fired! We demand an increase in funding for the minority student program!"

Aaliyah's newly formulated audience had a range of people. She met the eyes of students, faculty, administration, and surrounding homeowners. She wanted to keep going. "Today has opened my eyes to those who do stand for change. Those who are not afraid to push the boundaries of what is considered justice and how we can achieve equity in all institutions."

Aaliyah waited for the crowd's applause to cease. Aaliyah scanned the crowd to note the faces she saw today. Then her eyes landed on Charlie. She was beaming in the distance, standing by her lonesome. Her tall stature and red hair separated her from the crowd.

Aaliyah smiled from behind the megaphone. "We must grow within ourselves. Those who are here are the bridge between understanding and progression. So, if you're ready to continue inciting change, follow me!"

Aaliyah heard whoops and cheers as the crowd parted like the red sea for her. Jeremiah and Kiley fell in step with her, following her like the president's secret service. Aaliyah handed the megaphone to Kiley, and she began more chants. Aaliyah led the crowd of nearly four hundred people to the student union. People moving past the crowd on bikes and skateboards gave them cheers of approval as they moved to their destination.

Aaliyah breathed in the moment. Her heart was filled with joy for the first time in months and she felt purpose.

Aaliyah led the protestors to the student union in ten minutes. The ceiling of the surrounding buildings opened up in the middle of the union. The sun was shining directly on Charlie. She stood there with a wagon. In it was two cases of water, boxes of granola bars, and sacks of tangerines. Aaliyah took two steps at a time and knocked Charlie back with a forceful hug.

"Charlie! How'd you know I was coming here?" Aaliyah asked with a beaming smile.

"The protest was televised once the boys came out of the building. I gathered supplies for protesters immediately. I was wheeling over the wagon when I saw the news station cut off the news anchor and broadcasted your speech instead. I saw that I may need a few more supplies as people continued to arrive. Aaliyah, I just want to say I'm in awe of you." Charlie placed her warm hand on Aaliyah's shoulder.

Aaliyah put her hand on top of Charlie's and ways of apologizing swirled inside her head. Before she could, there was a tap on her shoulder. Jeremiah bent toward her ear, "I think they're waiting on you Ms. Harris," he winked and moved out the way to reveal the patient crowd staring at Aaliyah. Aaliyah looked back to Charlie and mouthed "thank you."

She moved to the center of the steps. With the shade provided by the buildings, she saw the news crew in the back with all black attire and baseball caps. Aaliyah saw the red light flashing and began, "The student union is the center of our campus because students are supposed to be the center of the university's focus. Yet many of us are ignored, dismissed and are not represented when it comes to faculty or administration."

Aaliyah was interrupted by a Black woman near the front, "That's right, baby!"

Aaliyah smiled. "So, I will stay here, at the middle point of Bellpoint University, until we are heard!"

The crowd cheered in response. Aaliyah waved Kiley, Jeremiah, and Charlie toward her. They all shuffled over awkwardly. Charlie tried to hide her rosy cheeks behind Jeremiah's broad shoulders. Aaliyah looked at her friends proudly. "I would like to thank those that are committed to being great allies." Aaliyah reached behind Jeremiah and squeezed Charlie's hand. "I've learned it's not only about educating yourself but allowing others to alleviate your burden."

Aaliyah turned back to the crowd. "It's the conversations we commit to at home and in the classroom. As this university expands, it cannot just grow economically; it must also grow in awareness and understanding. Our voices matter and don't let anyone tell you different!"

"Hey, hey! Ho, ho! These racist people have got to go!" Kiley shouted. Jeremiah joined after. Within a minute, the crowd joined the chant for a few minutes.

Aaliyah sat down on the top step. The crowd followed like she was their shepherd. Periodically, people would come to thank Aaliyah and grab a few items from Charlie's wagon.

One woman with a Bellpoint athletics T-shirt came up to the wagon, grabbed two water bottles, and spoke to Aaliyah. "Thank you so much for not giving up. I thought we lost back there."

"My family taught me that giving up is what they want us to do. As long as we stand together and continue challenging what is unjust, we will never see defeat."

The woman gave Aaliyah a kind smile and reached out her hand. "My name is Lyla. Hold on, I want you to meet somebody." She disappeared into the crowd and Aaliyah returned to her conversation with Charlie.

"Go on, Charlie." Aaliyah and Charlie snapped their heads up to the woman who had returned with a child.

Lyla crouched down to her child. "Tell them how old you are."

The little boy shyly looked at Aaliyah. "I'm four." He held out four small fingers.

Lyla continued, "And tell her what you told me."

The little boy flashed all of his teeth, "No justice! No peace!" He started to giggle.

Lyla scooped him up into her arms. "I brought him here today because I wanted to show him the injustices that occur all around us. I used to play basketball here, and as athletes we make so much money for the school. But I would see my African American or Latine teammates ask for necessities and be denied. Now, I donate to all the cultural centers to ensure they have the resources they need to support minority students. Seeing a center that my teammates saw as a second home on campus destroyed, almost destroyed me. My Charlie baby needed to see what true advocates look like." The mother rubbed the tip of her nose in her son's neck. They both shared a laugh.

Aaliyah stood up. Aaliyah was a step above her, but Lyla still towered over her at six foot four. Aaliyah grabbed Charlie's hand. "Hi, Charlie. Do you want some of my orange?"

Charlie's eyes grew, and he nodded his head rapidly. Everybody laughed. Aaliyah handed him a few pieces. "I know somebody else special named Charlie. You remind me of her."

Charlie ignored Aaliyah as he stuffed every piece Aaliyah handed him in his mouth.

The mother stepped down and looked at Jeremiah, Kiley, Aaliyah, and Charlie. "I commend you all. You are the future. Say bye-bye!"

Lyla adjusted Charlie on her hips. "Bye-bye!"

Lyla almost walked into the camera crew that were behind her on the steps. She swiftly avoided them with Charlie in her hand.

A deep baritone voice came from the man holding a microphone. "Excuse me, are you Aaliyah Harris?" He asked knowingly.

Aaliyah met him at the bottom of the steps and straightened her posture which made them eye-to-eye. "Yes, that's me," she stated confidently.

He gave a signal to the two men behind him with camera equipment. "Great! We're with the local news station. If you don't mind, we would like to conduct an interview of you."

Aaliyah looked behind him at the men setting up the tripod for their camera. The other was cleaning the lens. They both moved with ease.

The man got Aaliyah's attention again. "We just want you to restate the demands and discuss what you hosted today."

Aaliyah cut her eyes at him. "I'm not the host of anything. I am simply a student representing what minority students, in particular Black students, need."

The man held brief eye contact with Aaliyah. "Yeah, that's great. We want you to say all of that on camera."

Aaliyah felt her stomach cramp up. Her palms began to perspire, and her tongue felt like sandpaper. She felt she didn't know what to say all of a sudden. Aaliyah flattened out her top and ran her hand on her hair. While Aaliyah was adjusting herself, the man who approached her was quietly discussing something with his crew. She looked back to her friends for support, but they were all in their own conversation.

"I think she will have to do this interview another time."

A voice from behind Aaliyah cut off her scattered thoughts. The interviewer looked over his shoulder clearly irritated. He caught a glimpse of who was speaking, and his face quickly adjusted. "Oh. Um, good afternoon, President Carter." The man stepped back and almost tripped on his other foot.

Aaliyah turned around to face the person who had this man so distraught. Aaliyah was met with a White woman who was about five foot seven. She was dressed in a black pantsuit with forest green heels and gold spikes. Her hazelnut hair shaped her face in a nice bob that complimented her creamy, aging skin. Aaliyah remembered seeing her face on move-in day and in a few university emails.

She flashed a warm smile and reached out her wrinkly hand. "Hi, Aaliyah. I'm President Shirley Carter."

Aaliyah forgot basic functions for a second. *Reach your hand out, idiot!* she thought.

Aaliyah gave her a firm handshake.

President Carter looked sincerely in Aaliyah's eyes. "Aaliyah, would you like to meet with me and discuss some of the things you want to see change on this campus?"

It was as if the heavens had opened up and dropped down the perfect gift. "Yes, I would," Aaliyah responded too eagerly.

"Okay great, follow me to my office." President Carter spun on her heels and walked in the opposite direction of the student union. The reflection of the dimming sun shined on the gold spikes on her heels. The seated crowd noticed her walking up the steps and started booing. They hurled insults like they were throwing trash at the boys. Aaliyah heard comments of poor leadership and her not caring about her students.

President Carter clicked her shoes up to Kiley and crouched down. "May I use this, sweetheart?"

Kiley handed her the megaphone without a word.

President Carter walked to the center of the steps. She cleared her throat, "Good afternoon, Bellpoint community. I am President Shirley Carter. I understand the frustration of the past few days. First, I would like to offer my condolences to those effected. Today, I recognize we need a pivotal change. I am committed to engaging in conversations with students so I can hear the specifics of what we need to work on as a campus. I have asked this inspiring young lady, Aaliyah Harris, to be the first student I speak to. We will come out of this stronger than before!"

President Carter beamed after her declaration, but her smile quickly disappeared once she was met with the same blank stares as when she arrived. Aaliyah reached out for the megaphone and the President handed it to her with pale hands and an exhausted expression.

Aaliyah tried to stifle her laughter. She hid her smile behind the megaphone. "Thank you all for coming today.

We said we would stay here till our voices were heard and that's what we've accomplished today. I would like to urge everybody to never stop using your voice whether that's to amplify, support, or educate. Continue asking questions and being a critical thinker. We are nothing without each other and this university is nothing without us."

The crowd erupted in applause. They slowly stood up giving Aaliyah a standing ovation. She heard chants of her name and whistles throughout the crowd. Aaliyah heard groans from people stretching their stiff joints before they departed. A few people came up to her.

"Thank you for hosting such an organized protest."

"You will change the world!"

"You're such an eloquent speaker."

Aaliyah mastered how to say thank you and smile while she thought of what she wanted to address with President Carter.

"Huh?" Jeremiah asked.

Aaliyah shook her head. "What?"

Jeremiah chuckled. "I asked you what you're gonna say to the president and you said 'Thank you so much,'" he mimicked her practiced smile.

Aaliyah laughed. "I don't know. I zoned out thinking about it," Aaliyah gave him a worried look.

Jeremiah playfully punched her shoulder. "You'll know when you get there. Just remember to navigate the conversation. Don't let her control you. You know what you're talking about."

Aaliyah nodded. She felt like a star athlete getting prepared for an important game. "You're right. Oh! I think I'm going to need this." Aaliyah pulled on Jeremiah's backpack string. He slid it off his back and held it up for her.

Kiley looped her arm in Charlie's. "Good luck 'Liyah girl! We got yo' back."

Aaliyah pressed her hand to her lips and waved it to all her friends. "Thank y'all. I couldn't do this without you."

They all came in for a group hug. They laughed when Charlie bumped her head against Jeremiah's. Aaliyah stood there for a few seconds, happy. They all pulled away and Aaliyah adoringly watched them walk away.

President Carter had been stopped by a family wearing Bellpoint alumni T-shirts. Aaliyah recognized them as the parents at the sit-in with daughters who couldn't be above the age of ten. She walked closer but kept her distance so nobody would see her.

"...And now we're not sure where we should be sending our money!" The mother hissed.

"*Academic probation*? You've got to be kidding me!" The father was so angry, a few students walking by stopped their conversation.

President Carter countered their loud voices, "I know this last event has evoked poignant feelings for many proud alumni, but I assure you I will be taking into consideration all that students and alumni are saying. I have administration working hard here at Bellpoint."

The father's face relaxed when he looked at his daughters. He grabbed his one girl's hand and kissed it. "You better. Because if not, I will make sure my girls and my money go somewhere else." The family left grumbling more comments as they walked away. The mother gave Aaliyah a smile as she walked past.

Aaliyah gave the president a second to regroup before approaching her. She walked up slowly, pretending she hadn't heard her get torn apart.

President Carter turned to Aaliyah, "Okay! Ready? Did you say bye to your friends?" Her previous frown was replaced with bright eyes. Aaliyah sensed inauthenticity.

"Yeah." Aaliyah's long stride matched President Carter's quick pace.

"I'm very excited to talk to you, Ms. Harris."

Aaliyah couldn't say the same. So she didn't.

* * *

"Okay!" President Carter patted the notebook she took of Aaliyah's notes like she was congratulating a trained dog. Aaliyah stopped herself from rolling her eyes. President Carter leaned forward, "This is a great start, Ms. Harris."

She flipped her notebook around for Aaliyah to see. Aaliyah scanned her messy cursive to make sure she didn't miss any notes. President Carter used her pen as a cursor. "*So*, we have increasing the enrollment cap, financial and resource package for Black students, and…fire Dean Carter." Aaliyah looked up to see the president looking at her. Aaliyah shifted and distanced herself from the president.

"Aaliyah, honey, that last task is going to be a little more difficult," the President admitted sorrowfully.

"Why? Her son committed a racist act against your students, and you want that representation on your faculty?" Aaliyah persisted.

"Of course not, honey. It's more so the practicalities of removing somebody in that position. It's a long process. I just don't want you to think all of these will be completed by tomorrow," she admitted to Aaliyah.

Aaliyah carefully thought about her response. "You said you were going to make sure students feel safe on campus again."

President Carter furrowed her eyebrows. "Well of course!" she painted on a reassuring smile.

"Then in order for Black students to feel safe. She—" Aaliyah pointed behind her shoulder and looked President Carter in her eyes, "needs to go now."

President Carter sat up and awkwardly coughed. "I'll see to it that we search for an interim by the end of the month." President Carter glanced at Aaliyah as if a new person walked in her office. Her practiced smile returned, "Alright sweetheart, the office has been closed for over an hour and it's a new week tomorrow!" she told Aaliyah as she rose from her leather seat.

Aaliyah did not move her position. "Yes ma'am, I have class tomorrow, but I wanted to give you this before I left." Aaliyah gave her a sweet smile that dropped once she bent below the large wooden desk. She grabbed the stack of papers from Jeremiah's backpack. She stared at the papers, raised them perpendicular to the table and aligned them. "I took the liberty of creating a list of potential Dean of Students who will be considerate of *all* the students on campus."

President Carter fanned out the nine pages. "Oh…thank you," President Carter grabbed the paper hesitantly.

Aaliyah reached her long arm across the table. "This is the list of programs for Black student recruitment that I'm sure can be implemented for other students underrepresented on campus."

Aaliyah zipped up her backpack. "And on the other side of those essential lists are papers I'm sure would speed up the process of the new interim."

President Carter flipped over the papers and analyzed them as Aaliyah had that morning. The President's mouth gaped open. After reading all the messages she looked across from her to see a vacant seat.

Aaliyah stood at the door with Jeremiah's backpack rested on her shoulders. "I have a copy myself but I'm sure there's no need. Discussing things with you was great, President Carter. I hope to see progress soon." Aaliyah walked out of her office with a sinking feeling in her stomach. She wasn't sure if the threat was going to speed up progress or slow it down. President Carter had watched her leave with her mouth still hanging open.

Aaliyah got inside the elevators before she heard heels clicking from the office she was in.

"Tiffany! I need you to—" the office door slammed shut.

Aaliyah released a long sigh. On the ride down two floors, Aaliyah slid off Jeremiah's jacket and backpack. A trail of sweat had formed on the brim of her nose. Aaliyah stepped out of the building and gasped. The black cold night shocked her warm body. She put Jeremiah's jacket back on and held the backpack in her hand.

She began the journey to her dorm. Aaliyah focused her thoughts on the shower she would take and how warm her bed was. The entire walk, Jeremiah's backpack jostled against her knee. She switched hands and it did the same.

Aaliyah reached her dorm and scanned her student ID. Only one person was in the lobby. Aaliyah checked the clock that was flashing in bright red numbers in the center of the lobby.

7:43 p.m.

Aaliyah was so exhausted, she rested her body on the cement pole near the elevator as it creeped to her floor. She smiled to herself when the doors opened and nobody was inside. She stepped in and pressed six. As the doors closed

Aaliyah saw a hand sweep through the doors and had to keep herself from grumbling audibly.

The doors reopened to the Hispanic boy who was interviewed the day of the vandalism. He saw Aaliyah and smiled. "Sorry. I have an assignment due at nine that I have to get back for."

Aaliyah kept her eyes on the floor buttons. "No worries," she responded kinder than she felt.

The ride was silent. The only noise filling the space was their calm breaths and the beeps after each floor they passed.

Once they passed floor three, the boy turned to face Aaliyah. Fear caused her to step back. She tightened the grip around her keys. The boy stepped back once he saw her body tense up. "Sorry, I just wanted to say that I saw you at the open forum and the protest. You were very inspiring."

The doors opened and the boy held his hand out. "After you."

Aaliyah stepped out the elevator and walked down the hallway. She turned her head back to respond but she heard a door close. She smiled at an empty hallway. "Thank you," she whispered to herself.

Aaliyah unlocked her door and found Charlie reading a book on her bed with her headphones on. The music was playing so loud Aaliyah could clearly hear the words from the song she was listening to: "Arabella" by Arctic Monkeys.

Charlie took off her headphones once the light from the hallway shone on her face. "Hey," she greeted.

"Hey," Aaliyah replied. She started taking off the clothes she felt she had worn the entire week.

"I know you're not gonna leave me hanging. *How'd it go?*" Charlie urged Aaliyah. The headphone wire had gotten stuck in her hair, but her focus was on Aaliyah rather than detangling.

Aaliyah told Charlie about her encounter while moving about the room, gathering items for her shower caddy.

"Wow, so she took the suggestions?"

Aaliyah paused her response as she took off her shirt. "I don't know. We'll see in the next few weeks."

A beat passed. "So, what were those pictures of the text messages?"

Aaliyah turned to face the wall to take off her jeans. "Oh. They were screenshots of the messages between Wyatt and Dean Palmer and Wyatt's best friend in the frat."

Aaliyah heard Charlie's bed creak as she laid back down on her bed. "Oh okay. And you got those messages from—"

Aaliyah kicked her jeans to the side. "Grayson…"

Charlie picked her book back up.

An awkward silence filled the room. Aaliyah practiced what she was going to say to Charlie as the silence grew louder. She had figured it out and thrown her towel around her chest, but before she could tell Charlie anything, Charlie began to play her music again. Aaliyah looked at Charlie and saw her eyes quickly scanning each line of the book.

Aaliyah sighed and snatched up her shower caddy. She raised the shower caddy up past Charlie's book. Charlie peeked to the side of her book and gave her a quick thumbs up.

Aaliyah shuffled to the showers with her head down. She looked at the patchwork of the floor on her way to the bathroom. It was the best distraction she had from her overwhelming thoughts.

* * *

After spending an extra ten minutes in the empty showers, Aaliyah's shower shoes squeaked back to her room. Charlie was sitting up in her bed reading the same book, without her headphones. She snapped the book shut when she saw Aaliyah come in the room.

"Charlie, I wanted to tell you." Aaliyah leaned on her bed to face Charlie.

A look of heartbreak was on Charlie's face. "Then why didn't you? I broke it off with him. It wasn't even hard once I knew. Do you not think enough of me to think I would do that?"

Aaliyah took off her dripping shower cap and put down her caddy. Her hair products, African black soap, a toothbrush, and edge gel were staring back at her. She sighed. "That's not it at all. It's been hard ever since I've got here Charlie—"

"I know but—"

"No, you don't know. Just listen."

Charlie shut her mouth quickly. Aaliyah heard her teeth meet and she scooted back in her bed so her back was against the wall. She continued.

"I've never been where I may be the only Black person in the room. The transition from living with five Black people and going to predominately Black and Hispanic schools to a PWI and a White roommate was hard. Knowing that some people still have my best interest in mind, especially when it's evident many don't, was hard. You didn't deserve to be personally attacked but I need you to understand my hesitancy."

Charlie nodded. "I understand," she shrugged. "I just needed to know that I didn't do anything wrong or hurt you."

Aaliyah shook her head. "No, you didn't. Sometimes when I'm going through struggles that only Black people can relate to, I need to talk to Black people. There's comfort in relating to somebody through shared experience or a variation of such. Even if it is through trauma."

Charlie started to pick at her hangnail. "I get that. I was caught up in trying to do everything right and be the perfect ally. I didn't realize sometimes being the perfect ally means standing back and just supporting whatever you do."

Charlie looked up from her nails and hopped off her bed. She took a step across their small dorm room and wrapped her arms around Aaliyah. Aaliyah hugged her back. Aaliyah allowed the hug to linger even though she felt her skin getting drier by the second.

They both pulled away with genuine smiles on their faces. Aaliyah laughed and covered her smile with her hand. "I need to lotion my body before my skin turns your shade."

They both shared a laugh and went to bed.

NOBODY TELLS YOU: MENTORS ARE ESSENTIAL

———

Aaliyah, Jeremiah, Charlie, and Kiley arrived five minutes early for Professor Robinson's class. A couple other prompt students were in their chairs. They all laughed when Dr. Robinson looked shocked when they arrived at her class earlier than ever before.

"Good morning, Dr. Robinson," they all sang.

"Good morning, my wonderful students," she beamed back.

They found their way to their usual row and waited for the students to come spilling in. Like usual, Dr. Robinson didn't begin class until five minutes after it was scheduled. "We'll wait one more minute for any students making it across campus," she told them. Dr. Robinson continued setting up for the day's lecture. That was everybody's cue to continue their conversation.

Aaliyah and Jeremiah were laughing until the conversations turned into whispers. Aaliyah looked up at the door to see Grayson walking in with a black hoodie, gray sweatpants and slides without socks. She refrained from gagging after seeing his toes almost gripping the ends of his slides. He slipped into the classroom quietly with his hood on. Aaliyah couldn't tell why everybody was whispering, seeing that half the people in the class were dressed similarly to him.

Professor Robinson turned on the projector and it began to hum. "Good morning class. As usual, please take off your hats, hoodies, or anything else on your head that does not pertain to your culture." Dr. Robinson smiled while she scanned the room.

A few students near Grayson took a few glances at him as he didn't rush to take off his hoodie. Dr. Robinson noticed it too but continued anyway, "Today we're going to be talking about Critical Race Theory. We're going to discuss why some deem it as a necessity and others as a farce. Please pull out your notes from last week."

Aaliyah watched Grayson as everybody moved their heads down to pull out their notebooks and laptops. He sunk in his seat and twisted his head from side to side to see if anybody was watching. He slipped off his hoodie while students' noses were in their backpacks. Aaliyah gasped and slapped her hand over her mouth.

Everybody turned their heads toward her. She started pretending to have a cough attack. Aaliyah coughed so hard Kiley started swatting her back. Aaliyah instinctively held her hand up to stop. She got weird looks from some classmates but was saved by Dr. Robinson. "Last class we spoke about how race was a biological myth…"

Aaliyah swiftly kicked Jeremiah's foot underneath his desk. Without breaking eye contact with the projector, he started rubbing his foot with his other. Aaliyah clicked her tongue. She repeated the kick. Jeremiah curled his lip and flared his nostrils at her. She widened her eyes and discretely leaned her head in the direction Grayson was sitting. Jeremiah gave her a confused look. Aaliyah was the one to flare her nostrils this time. She got her ChapStick and rubbed a layer on her upper lip, pointing at the direction Grayson was sitting. Jeremiah turned his head back to the front of the classroom and quickly glanced to his left.

Aaliyah watched Jeremiah immediately put his head down with widened eyes.

"Ms. Harris, can you tell us what Azao said when he tried to gain citizenship?" Dr. Robinson asked with her head titled.

Aaliyah flipped through her notebook. She smiled at Dr. Robinson shyly. "I'm not exactly sure."

Dr. Robinson looked at Aaliyah for a second longer and turned to the class. "He said that race should not be accounted for when trying to gain citizenship. It should be based on their beliefs."

Aaliyah felt her cheeks heat up. She paid attention the remaining class time.

* * *

Aaliyah watched as students started checking their phones and zipping up their backpacks.

"Alright, we'll pick up on this next week." Dr. Robinson closed her textbook. Grayson was the first one out of the classroom. The rest of the students shuffled out of the lecture hall. The traffic jam built up as seventy students tried to squeeze through a single door. Aaliyah and her friends added to the last of the pile.

Aaliyah leaned toward all her friends and whispered, "Did you guys see Grayson?"

Jeremiah winced. Kiley and Charlie leaned forward. "Uh-uh," Kiley looked intrigued. Charlie shook her head.

"He had a black eye, and his hand was in a brace under his sweatshirt." Aaliyah pressed her lips together.

"Ms. Harris, can I see you for a second?" Dr. Robinson called out. She kept her eyes on the papers she was separating.

Jeremiah looked at Aaliyah and shrugged, "Maybe because you weren't paying attention in class."

Aaliyah tossed her hand, "Maybe so. I'll see y'all later."

"Bye." Charlie called.

"Later," Jeremiah smiled.

Aaliyah walked toward Dr. Robinson's desk. "Hi Dr. Robinson, you wanted to see me?" Aaliyah rocked back and forth on her heels and toes.

Dr. Robinson watched as the door creaked closed. She turned to Aaliyah, "Ms. Harris, I want you to have a seat."

Aaliyah furrowed her eyebrows but did as she was told. She sat in the front row, middle seat. Dr. Robinson typed on her laptop and a video spiraled as she made her way to the seat next to Aaliyah.

A young Black woman flashed on the screen. She looked to be around Aaliyah's age. She was wearing a black pencil skirt with a black blazer and purple button up shirt. She walked across the dimly lit stage and directly into the spotlight. She turned to face the audience after her confident stroll and began speaking immediately. "Nora Ephron goes into depths about some hard truths in a man's world. Ephron talks about issues many people are afraid to discuss at a graduation ceremony. She describes how we could strengthen this country by doing one thing: being aware. Taken from Wellesley College, Nora Ephron's Commencement Speech." The voice sounded like an adolescent version of Dr. Robinson's.

Aaliyah turned to her professor. Dr. Robinson smiled at the screen and pointed to it. Aaliyah reverted her attention back to the screen.

Aaliyah watched a young Dr. Robinson present a ten-minute speech about injustices in America. She moved across the stage elegantly and spoke with authority in her voice.

She's been captivating her entire life, Aaliyah thought.

The video ended with Dr. Robinson winning second in the National Speech and Debate competition of 1996. Aaliyah applauded alongside the 1996 audience. Dr. Robinson walked over and cut off the video. She pulled out the chair she taught in and sat down with one leg on the floor.

"Aaliyah, I was approached this morning by the assistant provost, and he asked me if I was interested in applying to be Dean of Students."

Aaliyah perked up in her chair.

Dr. Robinson took a pause. "And I immediately declined."

Aaliyah's shoulders sunk. "But Dr. Robinson, we need you. That's why I wrote your name down on that list."

Dr. Robinson gave Aaliyah a half smile. "Aaliyah, when I did my speech, that's when I knew I wanted to be an educator. I would educate myself and educate others just by the power of words, voice inflection, and pacing. I truly believe there is nothing like feeding knowledge to hungry minds."

Aaliyah nodded because she understood.

"I believe it's my calling to amplify and educate. I care for my students by doing so. *Not* by being a dean."

Dr. Robinson came over to Aaliyah and put her arm over her shoulder and placed her cold hand on Aaliyah's upper arm. "Do you understand, sweetheart?"

Aaliyah turned to her favorite professor. "I do."

Dr. Robinson shook her shoulder slightly. "Great!"

Dr. Robinson lifted up the projector screen and revealed an array of posters and flyers Aaliyah had never seen before. "I always keep the local speech and debate flyers posted in my room. I go and see the performers once in a while to show my support."

Dr. Robinson tore the tape off one flyer. "Something I see you doing very well in."

Aaliyah pointed to her own chest, "Me?"

Dr. Robinson handed her the flyer and chuckled. "Yes. I watched your statements in both the sit-in and the open forum. You have a gift, Ms. Harris, and I'm proud you're utilizing it."

Dr. Robinson extended her hand to help Aaliyah up. "There is another woman that I think would be a great fit for the Dean of Students that also participated in the open forum though."

Aaliyah hoisted herself up and thought about who she was referring to. "Oh!"

Dr. Robinson winked at her. "I have a class coming in soon. Have a great weekend, Ms. Harris. Can't wait to see your project next week."

Aaliyah smiled and walked out of the classroom with her backpack and flyer, feeling lighter than she had in a while.

* * *

"Hey, y'all," Jeremiah slapped his food tray on the table. "Sorry that took so long. I got a call."

"Oo, from who?" Kiley leaned in curiously.

"Bill Scott," Jeremiah answered.

Kiley scrunched her face. "Who's Bill Scott?"

"The director of the company that's rebuilding the BCC." Jeremiah turned to Aaliyah with his eyebrow raised.

Aaliyah turned away. "Don't look at me."

Jeremiah turned back to Kiley. "He called saying that I was recommended to assist in the image reconstruction for the center. He wants to take me on."

Kiley clapped her hands wildly. "That's great! You can add that to your lil' architect résumé."

Jeremiah swept his foot across the floor and blushed. "Yeah. I guess somebody's looking out for me." Jeremiah interlocked his pinky with Aaliyah's under the table.

Kiley got up from the table and threw her too-heavy backpack over her shoulder. "Alright you two, I have to get to Women's Studies. I'll see y'all later." She dove down to take one last bite of her sandwich before she emptied her tray.

Aaliyah and Jeremiah waved goodbye to her. Jeremiah's watch went off. He pulled back his crew neck sleeve. "Shoot, I forgot I need to go pick up some paint supplies from a friend. I need to start on Dr. Robinson's project today so the paint can start drying. I need to add to it throughout the week."

Aaliyah felt the loss of warmth as he scooted out of his seat. She put her chin in her palm and watched him get ready to leave. "What are you painting?"

Jeremiah looked up as he placed his beanie on his head. "You'll just have to be surprised, Ms. Harris." He winked at her and threw up a peace sign before he strode out of the cafeteria. Aaliyah threw herself back in the hard seat. She didn't know what she was going to do for her final project. She discarded her tray that hosted a finished strawberry banana smoothie and half of a blueberry muffin and walked out of the cafeteria with the sun beaming on her face. This time, she didn't shun it, she welcomed it. Aaliyah found a bench near the exit and sat her backpack down. She had twenty minutes before her next class began.

Aaliyah closed her eyes and let the sun meet her eyelids. She felt like someone was giving her a warm hug. Her phone buzzed in her backpack, and she fished it out of the front pocket.

"Hi, Momma," Aaliyah smiled at her phone.

"Hi, baby! You haven't called me in a week, so I wanted to check in on you." Her mother's voice sounded elated.

Aaliyah reflected over the past week. "Yeah, I'm doing good now. Sorry I didn't call." Aaliyah felt as guilty as she sounded.

"Well, starting Monday, it will be your last week of your first semester of college." Aaliyah could hear her mother's voice soften. She heard her sniff through the phone.

"Tina, don't start," Aaliyah heard her dad say in the background.

"Okay, I'm fine. Text me the dates of all your finals. I'll be up to pick you up the day after you're done."

"Okay. I'll see you on the fourteenth then." Aaliyah opened her eyes.

"Sounds good, baby. Remember to walk into each final with confidence! God is able and He has instilled you with the victory already! So claim it!" Aaliyah's mom said.

Aaliyah chuckled. She forgot how much she missed her mother's encouragement. "I will, Mom. Love you both."

"Love you too!" her parents said in unison.

Aaliyah got up from the bench and walked to the library. She walked along the crack between the dazzling sunlight and shade produced by the buildings. As she entered the library, Aaliyah saw a few people waiting in line for the elevator and decided to take the stairs. She walked up three flights of stairs before reaching the "Quiet Floor." Aaliyah walked between the dimly lit shelves. At the end of each aisle was a posted sign that read, "Please be silent on this floor. Eating can also be a distraction to others," under the last names of the authors. She ran her hand along the stacks of books and saw one of her favorite novels peeking out from the shelf. She gently picked it out of the shelf and gazed at it.

I know what I'm doing for this project now, she thought.

* * *

Aaliyah woke up the morning of the thirteenth at 7:15 a.m. She snoozed her alarm clock quickly so Charlie would stay sleep. She wiped the crust out of her eyes and stretched. Her long legs reached over her twin XL mattress swung to the ground as she yawned. Aaliyah patted herself on the back for organizing and packing her things the night before. When she had entered the room, Charlie was asleep on her desk, so Aaliyah had helped her to bed as Charlie grumbled profanities about how tired she was.

Aaliyah had spent five hours in the library every night the past week. She found a study round that was vacant each time she went. There would be days her scribbled, unfinished thoughts were left on the whiteboard from the previous night. She wanted to return to the library before her presentation so she could practice a few more times.

Aaliyah reached the same room and saw a message in another colored marker on the white board, "Happy Last Day of the Semester! Good Luck!"

Aaliyah smiled at the message. She slung her backpack off her shoulders and moved the desk to a corner. She took a deep breath and stood in the center of the study room. "The denial of justice cannot be…"

"And next up we have Jeremiah Anderson." The class gave Jeremiah a tired applause. He was the eighth presentation of the day and students were getting restless. Aaliyah, Kiley, and Charlie erupted in applause as Jeremiah jogged down the aisle to the front. He had his covered canvas in his right hand, while the other was swinging freely. Aaliyah admired how confident he always seemed.

Jeremiah brought his easel from behind Dr. Robinson's desk and smiled at her, nonverbally thanking her for letting him keep his easel in the classroom. She smiled at him from the front row with her infamous clipboard resting in her lap.

Jeremiah sat the painting down and stared at the black cloak covering his art. He turned to the class nonchalantly. "Good morning, class. As you've heard, my name is Jeremiah Anderson, and my final project is an art piece."

Aaliyah noticed a few students sit up in their chairs. Jeremiah's talent was known beyond communities he was involved in. He gently lifted the covering. The students broke out in whispered chatters.

"Wow!"

"That's amazing."

"I've seen his artwork before. He's really good."

That's an understatement, Aaliyah thought. Jeremiah revealed a painting of a Black woman with beautiful voluptuous natural hair. Her hair had words in it which depicted how Jeremiah described Black women's beauty. She was standing with her arms crossed over her chest, but her eyes were kind. Behind her read "Welcome Home!"

Jeremiah explained some of the intricate details of the painting like the hair description that some students inquired about. He flashed a smile at the class when his applause had much more enthusiasm than the student before. He walked back to his seat. Aaliyah felt the slight breeze as Jeremiah sat down. Kiley shook his shoulders swaying him side to side. Her mouth was wide open as if she were screaming on a roller coaster—that was her version of extreme praise.

People down the row and behind Jeremiah were all offering praises. Aaliyah watched him as he humbly thanked them all.

Dr. Robinson stood up from her seat and turned to the class. "Alright, that was the halfway mark through presentations. I'll give everybody a five-minute break to walk around, stretch, and chat. Get it out of your systems now because there will be no disruptions during the presentations. When we return from the break, Grayson Smith will be up." The class turned their heads toward the front-right side of the lecture hall. He embarrassingly sunk in his chair. Aaliyah could see his hands quivering from rows above. Students got up from their seats. Some moved around the class to chat. Others rushed to the exit to beat the bathroom line.

Aaliyah turned to Jeremiah, but he was already swarmed by new fans. Charlie walked around the crowd and took the empty seat to the left of Aaliyah. "I'm going to go fill up my water bottle. Wanna go?"

Aaliyah sucked on her teeth. "Uh, sure. I wanna stretch my legs anyways."

Charlie gave a weak smile. "Cool."

They walked out of the lecture hall at the same pace. Aaliyah noted how easily they both fell in step. She looked in every classroom they walked past. Every room was empty except one as students had completed their semester throughout the week. They reached the opposite end of the building. Charlie sat her water bottle underneath the dispenser, and it automatically shot cold water out.

Aaliyah shifted her weight side to side as she patiently waited for Charlie's water bottle to fill. Suddenly Charlie turned to her with a despairing look on her face.

Aaliyah grew concerned. "Woah, what's wrong?"

"I don't want to see him do his presentation."

Aaliyah threw her hands up in confusion and dropped them after she realized. "Oh."

Charlie swung her foot across the freshly mopped floor. "Aaliyah, he really hurt my feelings. I don't know if he was pretending to be somebody else or he's truly a coward. But it makes me ill with disappointment."

Charlie's face paled. They both turned their heads toward Charlie's water bottle as the water splashed from overflow. Charlie yanked it from the dispenser.

"Drink some," Aaliyah told her, pointing to the water bottle. Charlie complied and took one long slurp. Aaliyah tried to think of a solution as she watched the water recede.

Aaliyah hesitated. "Do you miss him?"

Charlie's eyes widened and she choked back some water in her bottle. "No! He just makes me upset. I can't even stand to see him in class." Charlie looked uncomfortable.

"I know this may not be what you want to do, but if you go back in the class and act unbothered, you ultimately have control over the situation." Aaliyah offered.

Charlie started doing light jumps in the hallway. "You're right."

Aaliyah hyped her up some more, "Because he lost out! It should be him feeling this way!"

Charlie's jumps went higher. "Exactly!"

"So, we're gonna go in there and barely give him any attention!"

Charlie slammed her water bottle down and a loud clanging sound bounced off the empty hallway walls.

A professor poked his bald head into the hallway. "Excuse me ladies! My class is taking their final. Do you mind lowering your voices?"

"Sorry sir," Aaliyah called out.

"Our bad," Charlie waved.

Aaliyah linked arms with Charlie, and they walked back to Dr. Robinson's class. Aaliyah pressed her ear to the door to hear any commotion. She heard soft murmurs of chatter and nodded to Charlie. Charlie swung the door open with both arms and walked in first. Aaliyah watched her freeze in motion, so she nudged her forward, and Charlie walked through the aisles with her head down. Grayson was at the front of the classroom with a paused video. Today, he was wearing jeans and a white button up with flip flops. His brushed hair and his stud earrings made him look more presentable than last the class. Aaliyah noticed the scars below his eye and chin healing slowly.

"So here's the video I created…" Grayson clicked play on his computer and jogged over to shut off the classroom's lights. He shuffled back to the front row seat next to Dr. Robinson. She patted his right knee.

A video clip began counting down from three. Clips of protests and cities ablaze flashed on the screen. The videos transitioned to pictures of Black neighborhoods destroyed by police in the 1980s. The photo faded into a picture of the destroyed BCC. The song "Change" by J. Cole was playing as audio. Students bobbed their head to the song. But Aaliyah knew the deeper meaning behind the melodic tune. The song cut out to a video of Thomas Sowell. The title read "The Ethnic Flaw 1984." The fifteen-minute clip described how Black people in America have insurmountable disadvantages due to racism being engrained in every institution. Sowell describes that despite this blatant discrimination, Black people continue to accomplish great things. Every student in the room was captivated.

The video ended and Grayson was standing by the light switch. He walked back to the center of the classroom while talking, "J. Cole is one of my favorite artists. This year, a special person—who I lost the privilege of talking to—made me recognize I cannot appreciate Black culture if I don't understand or educate myself about it," he stared at Charlie.

He tore his eyes away from hers and continued, "We're surrounded by Black culture but—like how our country treats African Americans—we neglect, disrespect, and remain ignorant in our ways. Like the title of the song, I'm trying to change too." Grayson ended his presentation in a small voice.

Aaliyah saw Charlie lean in with the same sad look in her eyes. The students applauded Grayson's presentation, but the reaction was not as enthusiastic as Jeremiah's. Aaliyah looked at Charlie and raised her hand.

"Yes, Aaliyah?" Dr. Robinson asked.

"I know you usually have a random generator for presentations, but may I go next?" Everybody on Aaliyah's row turned their head to see who volunteered.

"Of course." Dr. Robinson sat back in her seat and flipped to a new page on her clipboard. Aaliyah saw her scribble her name down as she made her way down the steps.

Aaliyah stood in front of Dr. Robinson's projector and moved it back a few inches. She took a deep breath and spun around on her heels. "Good morning, class. My project is going to be an interpretation of Bryan Stevenson's speech, 'We Need to Talk About an Injustice.' In this country we have this dynamic where we really don't like to talk about our problems. We don't like to talk about our history. And because of that, we really haven't understood what the things we've done historically have meant..."

Aaliyah walked around the room gracefully and with authority like she'd seen young Dr. Robinson do. She emphasized the points she wanted while softening her voice at points of nostalgia. She memorized every word of the nine-minute speech she interpreted. When she was done with her speech, Aaliyah waited for the applause to cease. Kiley, Charlie, and Jeremiah stood up and applauded her like she was a Broadway lead. A few students followed them until the entire class was giving her a standing ovation—even Grayson. Aaliyah bowed her head and felt her cheeks get hot. She looked at Dr. Robinson before she returned to her seat, and Dr. Robinson gave her an approving nod.

Aaliyah skipped up the stairs and felt relieved at being done with the semester and doing well on her project. Kiley was the next name on the random generator. She pulled a flash drive out of her pocket and placed it in Dr. Robinson's computer. On the projector, her title read, "The Future." Kiley presented on what direction she saw society going in ten years. She discussed the abolishment of prisons, credit scores, and race identification questions on all applications.

"As Mark Twain says, 'History doesn't repeat itself, but it often rhymes.' As long as we understand that these frivolous things in our society are the sole factors preventing us from equity, we can improve as one."

The class applauded Kiley's presentation. Aaliyah heard whispers throughout her presentation questioning the reality of abolishing prisons. Aaliyah was the last student to end her applause; she believed in Kiley that much.

Dr. Robinson stood up with her clipboard on her hip. "That was the final presentation of the semester. Wonderful work students. I have seen tremendous growth in every single one of you. I hope you continue to cultivate this curiosity and never stop challenging what you believe can be achieved. With mindsets like these, there are only heights to be reached, never limits. You are dismissed."

Students left their seats, but many moved to say their farewells to Dr. Robinson. Jeremiah put his finger through the strap of Aaliyah's backpack. "It's too many people. We have our meeting with President Carter in ten. We have to go," he said disappointedly.

Aaliyah looked at him with pleading eyes.

He chuckled at her expression. "You'll see her again."

Aaliyah and her friends exited the room that wasn't blocked up for the first time the whole semester.

NOBODY TELLS YOU: WELCOME HOME!

The morning light shone through Aaliyah's room. She turned to her side in bed and welcomed the light in. Aaliyah looked around the unorganized room decorated with open moving boxes, suitcases, and an overflowing trash can. Aaliyah hopped off her bed, narrowly avoiding her duffel bag which wouldn't zip the night before. She walked on her tip toes to her closet, careful not to wake Charlie.

Grabbing her shower caddy, she walked the empty hallway to the community bathroom and pressed play on her "Good Morning" playlist as she started to brush her teeth. After completing her morning routine, Aaliyah checked her phone. She knew her mother would flood her with messages about her arrival time. To her surprise, there weren't any text messages.

"I guess it's a good morning," she said to herself.

Aaliyah walked back to her room and opened the door quietly. She only remembered to breath once she heard Charlie's soft snores. She grabbed the tape that was on top of her dresser and closed a few boxes, stacking them on top of each other and scooting them in the corner. There was a soft knock at the door.

"Damn, the RA is already coming to pick up the keys?" she said softly.

Aaliyah swung open the door and gasped. It was her entire family.

"Hey *hey*, kiddo!" Aaliyah's dad scooped her up and squeezed her body in a hug.

Charlie jolted up from her slumber and dusted her unruly hair out of her face. Aaliyah's dad, mom, Damien, Keisha, and Ty entered the room. They all watched their step in the maze that was Aaliyah's room.

"I'm sorry, I thought you both would have been up and moving. I should have known this is morning to you." Aaliyah's dad grinned at his tired-looking daughter.

Damien looked around the messy room. "Dang, bruh! It's eleven o'clock. Whatchu been doing?"

Aaliyah leaped over her folded laundry basket and hugged her older brother. "Well, hello to you too."

"Hi, Mr. and Mrs. Harris. And hi, siblings. I promise I look more presentable when I've been awake for a couple more hours." Charlie smiled at the family.

"Hi, Charlie honey. It's so nice to see you again," Aaliyah's mom patted the edge of Charlie's bed. Charlie combed through her hair with her fingers once they turned back to Aaliyah.

Aaliyah's mother clapped her hands twice. "Harris family that came with me, we are exiting this room so the girls can have some more time to get organized. Move out!" Aaliyah's siblings did as they were told and moved out of the dorm room carefully.

Once all of them were in the hallway, Aaliyah's mom turned back to her daughter. "I got a moving bin for you already; it's in the hallway. It'll take us about fifteen minutes to pull the car around and I'll make the boys come back and help you load it up."

Aaliyah beamed at her mother. She wrapped her arms around her shoulders and squeezed, "Thank you, Momma."

Aaliyah's mom laughed and put her hand on top of Aaliyah's arm, "You're welcome, baby."

Aaliyah gently closed the door on her way out and turned back to Charlie. She was sitting up in her bed, still disheveled.

"Charlie, I'm so sorry. I didn't know they were coming—"

"Stop apologizing. I'm surprised my dad wasn't here at eight in the morning doing the same thing." Charlie waved Aaliyah's apology off.

Aaliyah chuckled and walked to open the door. She propped it open with her foot and reached into the hallway to drag the moving bin through the doorway. A couple students walked by their open door and peered in for a second. Aaliyah ignored the wondering eyes and placed her three moving boxes in the bin. She tossed her trash bag full of clothes and hangers in the bin on top of the boxes. She taped up her drawers that had all her essential items. She looked around the room for anything else she may need for her winter break at home.

Aaliyah watched the sun shine on her posters. The glare from the sun reflected on her dorm room keys. She snatched them up and put them in her backpack. Those few actions uncluttered the space. Aaliyah looked at the posters of Tupac, Frank Ocean, and Huey from *The Boondocks*. She chuckled when she stood back and saw that Charlie's posters of Paramore, Tame Impala, and Fleetwood Mac were directly across from hers.

Charlie got out of her bed and rose the blinds. She walked over to Aaliyah and they both stood facing the window, staring at their scenic view.

"What a semester. I was just hoping I wouldn't over-swipe my meal plan." Charlie commented.

They both looked at each other and started cracking up.

"Knock, knock," Aaliyah's dad and brothers appeared in the door.

"Hi, it's just that bin and I'm good."

Aaliyah's dad nodded, his smile never fading.

"Dang, 'Liyah! You're coming home for winter break, not moving out!" Damien complained.

"I have to switch out my summer clothes for winter. If you're too weak to move a four-foot bin with wheels, just say that," Aaliyah taunted back.

"Both of you, please! I got this," Ty's small frame appeared from behind Damien. He grunted a few times before the bin started to move.

"Thank you, Ty," Aaliyah leaned in and kissed the top of his buzzcut hair. The rest of the men followed down to the elevators.

Charlie laughed at the siblings' encounter. "Your entire family is beautiful. Makes sense," she gestured to Aaliyah's frame. Something began to buzz on Charlie's bed. She grabbed her phone. "Hey, Dad."

Charlie turned to Aaliyah with a smirk. "Oh, you're downstairs."

Aaliyah chuckled as she walked around the room, double checking she wasn't leaving any essentials.

"Okay, I'll come down in a few... Alright, bye." Charlie ended the call.

"Knowing my family, they're going to want to walk around campus and get some food. So, I'll text you after that and we can say goodbye?" Aaliyah said while making up her bed. She lunged across her bed to pull the sheets up.

"Yeah, that should work. I need more time to pack my things anyways. My dad and I will probably go to get lunch after that too." Charlie looked around her messy side of the room.

"Okay, I'll see you later." Aaliyah walked out of the room with her backpack and shower caddy in hand. She got downstairs, and Ty and Damien were playing on the lounge couch. Her dad was on the phone. Aaliyah assumed it was from work based on his unamused expression. Keisha and her mother were both chatting, the afternoon light shining on their melanin skin. Aaliyah took a mental picture of her family then approached them.

"Alright, I'm gonna put these in the car. Do we want to go get some food?"

Ty did his version of a cartwheel and ended with pumping his fist in the air. "Yeah!"

The Harris family chuckled at his burst of energy and followed Ty out the doors. Aaliyah felt an arm around her shoulder. "Well hello, Miss Bellpoint Tiger."

Keisha beamed up at her younger sister. Aaliyah saw that she had switched out her nose stud for a gold hoop which complimented her floral sundress and gold sandals. Aaliyah stopped in the middle of the walkway and hugged her older sister.

Keisha rubbed her sister's back and pulled away. "On the way home, you have to tell me all about your first semester."

Aaliyah shook her head at the thought. "Okay, it'll take the entire trip home too."

Keisha raised her eyebrow and scrunched her nose up. "Oh really?"

"Aaliyah!"

Aaliyah turned behind her to see where the voice was coming from. She smiled when she saw Jeremiah jogging toward her. "Hey," he said slightly out of breath. "I was about to ride home with the boys and saw you. I just wanted to say bye."

Aaliyah heard her dad excessively clearing his throat. She dropped her shoulders.

"John, kids, this is the nice boy Aaliyah, Ty, and I met on move-in day." Aaliyah's mom squeezed her husband's bicep and his tense muscles relaxed.

Aaliyah's dad stuck his hand out. "John Harris."

Jeremiah shook his hand, "Jeremiah Anderson. Nice to meet you, sir."

Damien gave Jeremiah a couple up-downs and held out his hand. "Damien. What's up, bruh?"

Jeremiah dapped him up and lunged forward when Damien yanked him in. Aaliyah watched as Jeremiah pulled back, opening and closing his crushed hand. "Nice to see you again, Mrs. Harris. And nice to meet you, Keisha?"

Keisha nodded and smiled, "Yes, nice to meet you too."

Jeremiah looked behind Aaliyah's mom, "Hey, little man."

Ty waved shyly from behind his mother's hip.

"Well, my ride is waiting for me. I just wanted to say good-bye and wish you all safe travels." Jeremiah hugged Aaliyah. She felt him slip something in her pocket. He took a couple steps back and waved one last time to the family.

Aaliyah's mom led the troop. She held on to her husband's arm and whispered in his ear. He was still tense from the previous interaction.

Keisha and Aaliyah laughed at their father and brother's reactions. "I hope he's the reason why your story is gonna take so long," Keisha smirked at her younger sister.

Aaliyah laughed and nudged her sister, "He's definitely part of it."

Their mom turned around from a few paces ahead. "Keisha! Look honey, they offer your major for graduate school. Both my girls could be alumni at the same school."

Keisha rolled her eyes and caught up to their mother. "Momma, we talked about this…"

Aaliyah fell back and watched her family walk the walkways she met her friends at. They passed the curb she and Charlie sat on their first day on campus. They reached the food area.

"Okay, if you want Jamaican, come with me. If you want salad, go with Mom." The boys zipped over to their dad's hip and Keisha remained with their mom. Aaliyah looked back and forth between each side then side stepped over to the boys.

"Alrighty, we'll meet back here to eat together," Aaliyah's dad confirmed.

When Aaliyah and the boys walked into the restaurant, they were hit with the delightful smells of jerk chicken, yellow curry, and rice. Ty tugged on Aaliyah's sleeve, "What do you get when you come here?"

Aaliyah looked down at her little brother. "This isn't on my meal plan, buddy. So, I don't usually come here."

Ty turned his nose up with confusion, "Oh."

Aaliyah laughed and pulled her phone out of her pocket, and something fell out of it. It was what Jeremiah had slipped into it. She picked it up and saw it was a flip book. Aaliyah flipped through pages of a picture of her own smile transitioning to laughter. The last page said "Aaliyah Harris" and was marked with the date they first met.

"Excuse me, ma'am. What can I get you?" The restaurant worker looked irritated at Aaliyah's obliviousness. The few people behind her look impatient as well.

"So sorry. Can I get the jerk chicken and coconut rice?" Aaliyah smiled at the flip book and held it to her heart. Once the rest of her family had food, they met her mother and sister at the table. Aaliyah had taken a couple bites of her food before she saw Dr. Robinson walking by.

"Dr. Robinson!" Aaliyah called with a mouth full of jerk chicken. Dr. Robinson stopped in her tracks and tried to identify where the voice was coming from. Aaliyah waved her over.

Dr. Robinson approached her family with a beaming smile. Aaliyah stood up from her seat. "Family, this is—"

Keisha dropped her fork on the table. She stood up, "Ms. Robinson!"

Dr. Robinson looked Keisha up and down with an open mouth. "Keisha Harris. I should have known." Dr. Robinson made her way around the table to hug Keisha.

Keisha turned to the family, "Ms. Robinson was my mentor after I interned with the Equity in Low Income Communities organization. I remember you telling me that you were going to go back and get your doctorate and return to teaching."

Dr. Robinson gave Keisha's shoulder a squeeze. "And that's exactly what I did. I knew I needed to influence young bright minds like you and your sister's."

Aaliyah cleared her throat, "Well I guess Keisha stole my introduction." The table laughed. Aaliyah looked at Dr. Robinson, "But Dr. Robinson is my favorite professor on campus. She encouraged me to step outside of my comfort zone this semester, while also making this place a second home."

Aaliyah's dad wiped his mouth with a napkin. "Well, thank you for taking care of my baby girl." He grabbed Keisha's hand. "Both of them."

Dr. Robinson looked at every person in Aaliyah's family, "It was my pleasure. I hope you all enjoy your break. I'll see you next semester, Ms. Harris."

* * *

Aaliyah held Ty's hand as they both skipped back to the car. Aaliyah giggled as he stumbled a few times trying to keep up with her pace. Ty led her all the way back to the navy-blue SUV they only took on road trips. Aaliyah ran her hand along the fading paint and smiled. Everybody started popping open the doors and hopping in.

"May I say bye to Charlie before we go?" Aaliyah asked her dad knowing he couldn't deny her pleading eyes.

He released a small sigh, "Go ahead."

Aaliyah's mom shook her head at his weak will with his daughters.

Aaliyah looked both ways before she dashed across the street. She scanned her student ID to open the dorm doors. Aaliyah stopped in her tracks when she walked inside the dorm lounge. Chills ran through her body as she saw Charlie and Grayson hugging. They stood there for a moment before Charlie pulled away. She looked at Grayson with hesitancy. Grayson said something that Aaliyah couldn't hear or make out. Aaliyah spun on her heels causing her shoes to squeak on the freshly mopped floor.

"Aaliyah!" Aaliyah could hear Charlie's steps quickly approaching her. Aaliyah quickened her pace hoping Charlie would give up.

Charlie caught up to her and grabbed Aaliyah's arm. "Aaliyah, wait."

Aaliyah moved her elbow out of Charlie's grasp. "Oh, hey."

Charlie looked back at Grayson, who immediately put his head down. "I know you saw that. He explained himself to me and I think he wants to do better. He seems like he actually wants to incite some change."

Aaliyah stepped back. "That's your decision, Charlie."

Charlie looked behind Aaliyah. "Where's your family?"

Aaliyah glanced at her shoes and looked back up at Charlie. "They're in the car. I was coming to say bye," Aaliyah squinted her eyes as the sun shifted directly in her face.

"Oh... Well, be safe. I'll see you in a month," Charlie said sadly. She closed the distance Aaliyah had created and wrapped her arms around her for a hug. Aaliyah hugged her back and stared at Grayson who was watching them. Aaliyah no longer wanted to look at him, so she pulled back. Charlie blocked her view of him.

"My family's waiting on me."

Charlie watched Aaliyah leave. "Bye! Be safe!"

Aaliyah walked slowly back to the car. She tried to process the feelings of betrayal and confusion. She got arrived and sat in her seat quietly. Aaliyah's dad turned around in his seat, "You say bye to your friend, chickpea?"

Aaliyah nodded at the ground and put on a fake smile. "Yup."

He started the car. "Harris family is out!"

Aaliyah pulled her phone out from her pocket and sent a text:

Be safe.

Aaliyah and her family rode down the streets on their way back home. Their bodies jostled in the car when they rode over a pothole. Aaliyah chuckled to herself and smiled out the window as they passed her dorm.

Maybe this is home after all, she thought.

ACKNOWLEDGMENTS

First, I would like to thank God. I prayed for an opportunity to have my voice be in a tangible body of work and He never fails to show His power. To You be the glory.

Nana and Grandpa, the first thing I do when I pray is thank Him for you both. Thank you for your love and encouragement during this journey. I love you so much.

Mom, thank you for never missing a moment. From every game to every crying call, you are the epitome of patience and love. I love you, Momma.

Dad, thank you for encouraging me to reach for the stars. You inspire my voice and continue to help cultivate it. I love you.

Kyla, my best friend. Thank you for being everything I need and more. The Blaylock sisters reach highs, never limits. I love you.

To my beloved beta readers, Andrea Linan, Alexandria Hightower, Kimberly Carter, and my Uncle Lance. Thank you for making this story better than one mind could make it. You each have had a hand in shaping a facet of my being. I can never thank you enough.

A special thank you to my wonderful supporters:

Aashna Bombwal
Alice Kennedy
Alexia Oduro
Andrea Allison
Andrea Linan
Angela Allison
Angie Garcia
Asha Patrick
Avery Evans
Bernadette P. Somera
Beverly Ntagu
Bobbie Trotter
Brandon Magee
Caitlin Szikszai
Camryn Lotka
Carla Carangue
Carmen Waterford
Carolina Buzato Marques
Charlie Faas
Chris Gunnett
Christina Siangco
Cimone Manson
Cynthia Gibson
Darriell Mason
David Smith
Debby Couture
Debra McLaren
Delfina Glover
Diana Fieck
Elijah Fletcher
Ejypt Gates

Alex Castro
Alexandria Hightower
Amira Moore
Andrea Clater
Andy Feinstein
Angelica Espinoza
Anita Bradley
Ava Montgomery
Belita Butler
Bettye Peterson-Sykes
Bhargavi Garimella
Bonnie Reddick
Brianna Somera
Camila Santiago
Cardellia Hunter
Carla Patrick
Carol Watson
Celia Luna
Chike Amobi
Christina Perri
Christine Borrero
Clark Moses
Cynthia R. Williams
Dauphine Logan
DeAnna Barrett
Deborah Williams
Decemeegan Togatorop
Derrick Burnside
Duane Michael Cheers
Ella Downs
Emily Shepard

Erin Mormion

Eric Cross

Eric Koester

Felicia Barmer

Frank Harris

Fraol Olyad

Gianna Rivera

Giovanni Rivero

Greg Watkins

Harold Moore

Isabel Stuber

Jabari Garnett

Jacqueline Van Liefde

Jamila Lawyer

Jennifer Cunningham

JoAnn Hill

Joy Moore

Julie Thomas

Kalkidan Worku

Karen Howard

Karlen Davis

Kathy Galloway

Katy Davis

Kendrick Dial

Kevin Watson

Kimberly Carter

Kriza Casem

Kyla Osborne

Lance Wedlock

Lauren Sykes

Lee Barreto

Ethel Mary Daniels

Eric Hansen

Evan Dennis

Francesca Levett

Frannie M. Narcisse

Gabrielle Mirand

Gina Hunnicutt-Booth

Grace Rector

Hannah Adair

Harold Trotter

Isaiah Robinson

Jacqueline Blaylock

James Herrick

Jaretzi Vargas

Jessica Chavarin

Joelle Cox

Julianna Edgerly

Kaila Oliver

Kara Lee

Karina Delgado

Kathryn Snyder

Katie Lafferty

Kaylee Broadhead

Kendyll McHenry

Kim Kaufman

Khyri Jones

Kyla Blaylock

Kyra Alsisto

Laura K. Randall

Laurie Russell

Lexi Olmsted

Liana Ordonez

Linda Martin

Lorena Miranda

Maddie Anyaji

Marcia Harris

Mariano Perez-Appel

Mary Castleberry

Maureen Dotson

McKenzie Justus

Melodee Thomas

Michael Wiafe

Millicent Scott

Monique Brooks

Natalie Roberts

Nicole Eliaschev

Noor Albandar

Patrice Braswell

Patricia Oyeshiku

Quebet King

Regina Bishop

Rochelle Hickman

Sal Terrones

Sandra L. Peterson

Scott Sucliff

Shanise A. Dews

Shaun Fletcher

Shelee Petka

Shianne Turner

Sohil Kshirsager

Spencer Torres

Stephanie Anyaji

Linda Anthony

Lisa Vlay

Mabel Dugbartey

Maddie Serrano

Maria Elena Googins

Marlenne G. Carrillo

Mary L. Matthews

Maurice Harris

Mecca Horton

Micaela Davis

Michelle Ford

Mina Fuentes

Naomi Waldron

Natashia Townsend

Nicolette McGaugh

Olivia Sammond

Patrice Lee

Pele Drayer

Quinada Ruffin

Robert Wedlock

Ryan Pope

Sandra Cook

Sandra Page

Seth Mallios

Sharon K. Ricks

Shelby Gordon

Sheryl P. Johnson

Shirley M. Zavala

Solé Ortiz-Ruiz

Staajabu Heshimu

Steve Schnall

Sydney Schauble	Taryn Smith
Tasia Carter	Terri Syktich
Tess Johnson	Thanh-Thao Sue Do
Timothy Shaw	Trinity Holloway
Tristyn Thomas	Valencia Morris
Valerie Morris	Vanessa Colonia
Vicki Neill	Vincent Anthony
Willie Blaylock	Yasmine Blaylock
Zackary Albrecht	

Thank you all for following Aaliyah's journey. I hope she inspired you to challenge the debilitating norms in our society and aim for more inclusivity. We will have a brighter future if we let love be our guide rather than the discriminatory values that seem to ground us as much as gravity does. We are bound by the ideas we perpetuate, not by institutions. I hope *The Story They Never Tell Us* inspires you as many books have done for me.

Made in the USA
Middletown, DE
20 December 2021

56339442R00106